"Relationshi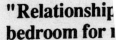 bedroom for i

Tyler's smile faded ... that?" Their kiss was still fresh in his mind.

Cass drew a deep breath. "Then why are you bothering with me?"

"Now you're the one being obtuse." He kissed her again. Hard. "I happen to have one hell of a reaction to you—and you to me—and it definitely isn't platonic."

She pushed him away. "Tyler, it's not hard to figure out the kind of relationships you've had before—no strings, no attachments, no commitments." *And no kids*, she added silently. "Let's face it. I know what happens when two people don't want the same things. We're just too different."

"That's not necessarily bad." He smiled knowingly.

"I don't need any more complications in my life."

"You mean complications of the male variety?"

"*Especially* the male variety."

Dedicated to Pat Kennedy

Like a Lover

SANDRA JAMES

MILLS & BOON LIMITED
ETON HOUSE, 18-24 PARADISE ROAD
RICHMOND, SURREY TW9 1SR

First published in Great Britain in 1992
by Mills & Boon Limited, Eton House, 18-24 Paradise Road,
Richmond, Surrey TW9 1SR

© Sandra Kleinschmit 1992

ISBN 0 263 77945 9

21 - 9209

Made and printed in Great Britain

1

"YOU," accused a flat feminine voice, "have gone crazy."

Behind the screen of his *Wall Street Journal*, Tyler Grant uttered a silent prayer that his uninvited guest would leave. He'd moved into his new house less than a week ago; Suzanne had been here the last two days. She'd been sweet and cajoling at first, but Tyler wasn't fooled. She'd hoped to try once again to convince him how wrong he'd been to make the move here to Crystal Lake. And as usual lately, a little of Suzanne went a long, long way.

"So I've been told." It was difficult keeping the bite from his tone. "By my friends. By colleagues—"

"*Former* colleagues!" Suzanne pointed out sharply.

Behind the newspaper, Tyler smiled. He liked the sound of that. It reminded him that he was totally on his own now, with no one to account to but himself.

He folded the newspaper and placed it on the desktop. Suzanne was a stockbroker for one of the top brokerage houses in Chicago. The securities firm Tyler had worked for did a great deal of business with them.

She stood before him, dressed in a sleekly fitting scarlet skirt and jacket. Matching pumps encased her feet. Her dark hair was pulled into an elegant twist on top of her head. Her makeup was flawless, as usual.

Suzanne was, Tyler admitted, a woman who had a lot going for her. She was beautiful. Smart and savvy. The two of them were friends; once they'd been lovers. Marriage had never been a serious consideration for either of them. Suzanne had her priorities already set out, and a husband wasn't one of them. Money came first, along with power and prosperity, which suited Tyler just fine.

To Suzanne, success meant a luxurious high-rise condominium on Lake Shore Drive, plush carpeting, walls covered with paintings and a guard at the door. For a long time Tyler had felt that way, too. But somewhere along the way all that had paled.

He'd been a professional trader on the Chicago Mercantile Exchange for ten years, and at the last, he'd felt every one of those years. Few people understood the tensions, the pressure and the stress of the Chicago exchange. True, there were fortunes to be made—and fortunes to be lost. It was a world of overnight millionaires, filled with electric fascination, dizzying and pulsating.

It was also a world of hard drinking and broken marriages. Tyler had seen too many men driven to the edge—by success, as well as failure.

It had been exciting and rewarding while it lasted, but the day had come when Tyler realized a lifetime dose would surely smother him. His life had lost its luster—and so had Suzanne, even then.

Gold bracelets jangled noisily as she moved forward and slapped both hands flat on the desk top. "How can you do this?" she demanded. "Tyler, you've been one of the top traders in Chicago for years! Oh, I know how hectic and frantic the exchange can be. I hoped that cruise you took would put you back on track...."

Now there was something to smile about. He'd spent four heavenly weeks in May sailing the Caribbean, doing absolutely nothing. It had been bliss, pure bliss. But even then, he had already known what he wanted and he wasn't about to change his mind.

Scarlet-tipped nails tapped out a staccato rhythm on the desk. "You're a survivor, Tyler. Don't you know that? Stocks and options are in your blood! But now you're throwing everything away!"

A cold wet nose nudged his hand. Tyler glanced down and saw the newest addition to his household, a Shetland sheepdog puppy named Missy. The pup gazed at him mournfully. Tyler's brown eyes softened. He lifted the dog onto his lap, remembering how Suzanne had fumed for an hour yesterday over the black-and-white hairs she'd found on her slacks. From the corner of his eye he saw that she was fuming once more at his lack of attention.

"Stop exaggerating," he said cheerfully. "I haven't dug a hole and buried my head in the sand forever. Besides, you sound as if I've chucked it all completely, when you know that isn't true."

Suzanne clearly wasn't inclined to share his good humor. "So you're really planning to go through with this? Putting out an investment newsletter? Doing a little consulting?"

The disgust in her tone didn't go unnoticed by Tyler. His smile vanished.

"I have the finances," he informed her evenly, putting a hint of the ruthlessness that had stood him so well in his years as a trader into his voice. "I have the know-how and I have the contacts to make this newsletter a rip-roaring success. Or maybe you're just upset because I didn't ask you to be a partner."

"Oh, I'm not doubting your ability to make another killing. But here? In this little town? I don't understand you, Tyler." Her soft, pampered hands landed on her hips, and she sniffed disdainfully. "You could have had a beach house in Florida. A condo in Hawaii! Or at least a vacation place in Lake Geneva! I still can't believe you actually bought this—this monstrosity. It's big, but it's so—so humble!"

Humble. Tyler's fingers tightened in the snowy-white fur that ringed Missy's neck. Humble was something Suzanne definitely *wasn't*.

He pushed back his chair and put the pup back onto the floor. Rising to his feet, he offered Suzanne a tight little smile. "Two things, Suzanne. I don't need an office like yours to get this newsletter off the ground. All I need is a little peace and quiet. Second, in case you hadn't noticed, this is Wisconsin, not the wilds of Alaska. Chicago is only an hour's drive away, which reminds me—" he rounded the corner of his desk and glanced pointedly at the door "—you'll run into rush-hour traffic if you don't leave soon."

Miraculously, his words finally had the desired effect. Suzanne jammed her purse under her arm and stalked from the room. Tyler followed at a more leisurely pace. At the front door she whirled around.

"You know you're going to hate it here! You'll be back, Tyler, I know you will. You'll be back in Chicago by the end of the summer at the latest!"

More than anything, he wanted to murmur a smug "We'll see." But he didn't, because that would only have prolonged their encounter. He shrugged and opened the door for her.

She passed through, visibly in a huff. He heard the rapping of her heels down the wooden porch, all the way down the sidewalk and onto the driveway.

She stared him down over the top of her blood-red Mercedes-Benz. "Tyler?" she called sweetly.

His eyebrows quirked in silent question.

She yanked the car door open. "I hope you're allergic to that damned dog of yours!"

The door slammed. The engine roared into life. The car zoomed off with a squeal of tires.

Tyler held back as long as he could. A chuckle emerged, then a full-blown laugh that came from deep in his belly. He was still laughing when he collapsed behind his desk again a minute later.

"God, that felt good," he said. Why, he hadn't laughed like that since . . . he couldn't even remember when.

Beside him, the puppy's tail swished madly back and forth. Tyler laughed again and reached down to scratch her behind the ears. "You approve, too, huh?"

Missy trotted over to the French doors leading onto the deck, her nails clicking on the polished oak floor. She stopped and looked back at him expectantly.

Tyler rose. "Time to go out, eh?"

Missy wagged her tail in agreement. As soon as he opened the door, she ran across the wide redwood deck and bounded down the steps.

Tyler trailed behind her, but paused near the deck railing.

The view was one he'd never grow tired of. Dazzling June sunlight blazed a sparkling trail across the surface of the lake that was the town's namesake. Stands of cottonwood and oak dotted the shoreline, deep and green against the backdrop of the sky. A small, secluded inlet lapped the edge of his property. There was even a boat dock.

The minute the realtor had shown him this house earlier in the spring, Tyler had known this was the one. Suzanne had called it a monstrosity. He called it rambling, with rooms so big he could hear his voice echo. Suzanne had called it humble. He called it charming. Suzanne would only have been satisfied with an elegant glass palace, but to Tyler, this house was all he'd ever wanted. Not one, but two massive stone fireplaces. Lots of trees and homey warmth. It hadn't mattered that this was the only house on the block to boast lake frontage. That was just a bonus.

And Suzanne thought he'd be back in Chicago by the end of the summer? "Never in a million years," he scoffed.

Somewhere nearby, Missy yipped. Still smiling, Tyler followed the sound around the corner of the house. His office angled out from the downstairs living area; the other side of the house had a huge recreation room and bedrooms upstairs.

He came to a halt in front of his office window. Missy was sniffing along the roots of a huge hedge that separated his property from that of the nearest neighbors.

Oh, yes, he thought with a swell of satisfaction. The frenzied pits of the exchange were light-years away. He could go to bed at night without having his head still roaring from the constant din. True, he wasn't much of a cook; he'd eaten out most of the time in Chicago. But he had everything else; time to work at his leisure and time to play. Here he had the peace and quiet he'd always craved....

An earsplitting screech rent the air.

Tyler's head jerked up. Missy's ears pricked forward. "What the . . . ?"

He rushed forward and shoved aside the hedge with both hands. His neighbor's yard came into focus, a kaleidoscope of shapes and colors. He dimly registered a sandbox in the corner, a swing set, a small patio strewn with push toys. As he watched, a string of small children rushed out the patio door.

It was then he noticed a slow curl of something drifting lazily from an open window....

Smoke.

"Hurry!" cried a voice that was unmistakably youthful. "Come on, everybody outside!"

Tyler didn't wait any longer. He vaulted the fence leading to the front and bolted next door.

CASS LAWRENCE tapped her fingers impatiently against the steering wheel while she waited for the light to turn green. She was anxious to be home, and with good reason.

She hadn't been comfortable leaving her oldest daughter Katie home with a brother, one sister, and three of the other children she had agreed to baby-sit for the summer. But as Katie had pointed out, it was only for a few minutes.

"I'm really sorry I walked through that poison ivy, Mommy," whispered a tiny little voice beside her. "And I'm sorry I put all those diapers on Kitty."

Cass looked down. Mournful blue eyes stared into hers. Five years old, Trisha was the youngest of her four

children. Also, Cass thought wryly, her most devilish
and talkative.

Because of Trisha, on several counts, Cass had had
to make an unexpected run to the drugstore. Trisha and
her brother had been playing near the lakeshore, and
Trisha had managed to walk through a patch of poison
ivy. Her ankles were so red and itchy that Cass had had
to phone the doctor. He had called in a prescription, but
unfortunately the drugstore closed at five today, so
she'd had to leave the kids in Katie's charge. To make
matters worse, earlier this afternoon Trisha had
sneaked all of Emily's disposable diapers from her diaper bag—and used them all on her doll Kitty. When
Cass went to change Emily after her nap, she discovered the diapers were missing. But at least she hadn't
had to make another special trip to buy more diapers.
Luckily the drugstore carried the kind Emily's mother
used.

She dropped a kiss upon her daughter's blond head.
"You're forgiven," she said lightly. "But remember you
are not to be down at the lake unless Mommy's along.
And we're going to have to make sure you know what
poison ivy looks like."

In the back seat, toddler Emily thumped her fists and
let out a squeal. The other kids Cass sat for were all of
school age. It would work out well for all of them, since
the kids would go back to school in the fall. At first
she'd been a little reluctant to take on Emily. But Emily
was a sweet-natured baby, and her mother understood
that she'd have to find another sitter in September.

After all, Cass would go back to her job as teacher's
aide at the local junior high school. For now, school was

out for the summer. And she had to supplement her income somehow. . . .

The light turned green, and Cass stepped onto the gas pedal. Moments later she turned onto a tree-lined street. Warm wind flowed through the window, whipping her bangs into her eyes and pulling several strands from her ponytail. Cass brushed the reddish-gold curls aside and released an involuntary sigh of envy.

There at the end of their dead-end street was the Campbell place—only it wasn't the Campbell place any longer.

The new owner had moved in just this week. Linda across the street had told her that some big-shot financier from Chicago had bought it. Cass hadn't seen Mr. High-Roller yet, but she hadn't missed the gleaming red Mercedes-Benz parked in front of the house the last few days. She'd dubbed the car's owner Ms. Sexy Brunette.

It *was* a house Cass could sink her teeth into, though. She'd been inside it only a few times, but she'd fallen in love immediately. It was a few years newer than the rest of the standard, ranch-style homes on the block and set back among the trees. The rooms were huge, with gleaming hardwood floors and pine-accented paneling. The kids had gone wild when the Campbells put it up for sale.

"Why don't we buy it, Mommy?" Eight-year-old Samantha had gazed up at her pleadingly.

"Yeah!" Katie's eyes had lighted up like lights on a Christmas tree. She'd sent a speaking look toward her two younger sisters. "Then I wouldn't have to share a bedroom with Sam and Trisha!"

Todd had spoken up, as well. "There's a stairway that leads down to the lake, Mom, but Old Man Campbell would never let any of us through to go swimming! If we lived there, we wouldn't have to ride our bikes all the way down to the public beach!"

Cass had sent her ten-year-old a warning look, though she'd silently agreed with his assessment of their former neighbor. "You shouldn't call him Old Man Campbell," she'd said sternly, "even if he has moved away. Besides, would you want the whole neighborhood cutting through your backyard to go swimming? After all, the beach is only four blocks away."

"But it's not the same as swimming in your own backyard! And everybody called him that, Mom!"

Cass winced at the memory. A three-bedroom house with four kids did cramp the girls' sleeping arrangements. Katie was old enough now to want some privacy from her younger sisters. Unfortunately, Cass had little choice in the matter. They'd lived in this house since Katie was a baby, and the mortgage payments were cheap by today's standards.

No doubt the kids were as tired of hearing, "We can't afford it," as she was of saying it. But things hadn't been easy since Rick walked out on them nearly two years ago.

Cass had schooled herself to feel nothing whenever she thought of the man who had been her husband for fifteen years. But it was at times like now—times when she saw how difficult he'd made things for the kids— that she was filled with a burning resentment.

She'd run the gamut of emotions since Rick had left her—hurt, fear, denial and anger. For a while she'd even hoped he would come back. She had been so scared then, so frightened and uncertain, a woman alone, with no marketable job skills and four children to raise and support. Caring for her home and family was really all she knew....

But she had coped, and because of that, she was a much stronger woman now. There were still times when she felt a touch of apprehension. But she was also very determined, maybe even a little stubborn, and knew those qualities made up for whatever she lacked in self-confidence.

Angling the car into her driveway, she glanced anxiously at her watch. She'd been gone less than fifteen minutes. Surely nothing had happened during the time she'd been gone. So why did she have the feeling something *was* wrong?

She got out and reached back to unbuckle Emily. Lifting the toddler to her shoulder, she reminded herself once more that Katie was a very mature and responsible fourteen. She'd sat for some of the neighbors since she was twelve.

On that note, she started toward the house.

Trisha clutched at her free hand. "What's that funny smell?" she asked curiously.

Cass stopped short. Her nose lifted instinctively. There was a pungent, acrid odor in the air....

Good Lord! It was smoke!

2

THERE WAS A FIRE, all right. But, thank God, it wasn't more serious.

Tyler wiped his forehead with the back of his hand and succumbed to a feeling of pure relief. Hell, his heart was pounding as if he'd run a three-minute mile. The girl he'd heard yelling had pointed him inside the house, screaming that the utility room was on fire. Sure enough, there were flames shooting from the electrodes on the top of the water heater there. Luckily, the girl had run into the garage and found a fire extinguisher. Moments later, Tyler had the flames completely doused.

He set aside the fire extinguisher and turned to survey his audience. The kids—every last one of them—had moved from the patio and now crowded near the utility room's outside entrance. Their faces were no longer frightened; they appeared more curious than anything else. He hinged the screen door open to let out the room air and propped his shoulder against the doorjamb.

"Gee, mister, you did that like a pro. Are you a fireman?"

Tyler shook his head. The boy who spoke had the same honey-gold hair as the oldest girl. From out of nowhere a most outrageous thought flitted through his mind. Surely *all* these kids weren't brothers and sisters? They appeared to range in age from about seven to thirteen or so, but what did he know about kids? And no one these days had kids *that* close together...or did they?

He summoned a weak smile. "Actually, no. I'm not a fireman. I'm a—" He stopped abruptly. Would these kids have any idea what he was talking about? "I'm in finance," he finished lamely.

"Oh." The boy looked doubtful. He jammed an elbow into the oldest girl's side and ducked his head.

She heaved a sigh of impatience. "It has to do with banks and things like that, Todd."

"*Oh.*" The boy gazed at Tyler with renewed interest.

Tyler cleared his throat. "I...ah, I'm your new neighbor—Tyler Grant."

"You bought the Campbell place?" The boy's eyes shone eagerly.

Tyler glanced back at his house. "That's right," he said.

"I'm Todd Lawrence." The boy nodded toward the oldest girl. "That's Katie. She's fourteen. She doesn't like to smile, though, 'cause she just got braces a month ago."

Katie swung a hand at him.

The boy laughed, neatly sidestepped and pointed to the rest of the group, one by one. "This is Samantha, Brian, Sara and Dave."

Tyler winced. Todd's admiring gaze made him feel guilty as sin. He really had nothing against children, but if he'd known there were six children living next door...

He closed his eyes for an instant, convinced this was all a horrible dream, that when he looked again, they'd be gone.

Good heavens, they were still there... all six of them.

There was an awkward pause. "How come you kids aren't in school?"

Six pairs of eyes looked at him as if he'd sprouted a nose like Pinocchio's. There were guffaws and titters all around. "Yesterday was the last day of school," someone announced triumphantly. "We're off for the rest of the summer."

Stupid question, Tyler chided himself silently. But at least he knew where these sweet little darlings had been when he'd first looked at his house in March. *It's a very quiet neighborhood,* the realtor had said. That it was, Tyler admitted reluctantly... when school was in session.

"Boy," Todd said matter-of-factly. "It's a good thing Trisha and Emily weren't here when this happened. Trish would have screamed bloody murder. She won't even go near the oven when Mom opens it."

Trisha and Emily. There were two more? Tyler felt as if he'd been blown into the center of a raging storm. He still hadn't recovered from the shock of the first six!

But the boy's statement made him wonder, and one thought gave way to another. Exactly where, Tyler thought grimly, was Mom?

Somewhere in the house a door slammed sharply. He heard the sound of running footsteps. By the time Tyler turned around, he found himself face-to-face with an older, more mature, and infinitely more harried-looking version of Kate.

This, he suspected, was Mom.

CASS SAGGED against the doorjamb, rife with disbelief. Muddy-looking streaks darkened the sunny-yellow walls of her utility room. Though the outside door stood open, the smell of smoke lay thick and heavy in the air.

"We had a fire, Mom! We smelled smoke right after you left."

A fire! Cass's head was whirling. She clutched Emily desperately. Emily wiggled a protest, but Cass scarcely noticed. "My God," she said faintly. "I was only gone fifteen minutes...fifteen minutes. And this happened?" Her eyes darted to the group still clustered on the patio outside. "Is everyone okay?" Her gaze slid to the tall form shadowed in the doorway.

Tyler decided she might as well have vented her thoughts through a loudspeaker. *Who on earth are you,* she was thinking, *and what are you doing in my house?*

He stepped forward and offered his hand. "I'm your new neighbor, Tyler Grant. I ran over when I saw the smoke."

So this was Mr. High-Roller from Chicago. Where, Cass wondered fleetingly, was the impeccable three-piece pin-striped suit? The stuffed-shirt image she'd somehow expected? This man wore simply cut but perfectly creased wheat-colored slacks. A crisply pressed shirt emphasized wide shoulders and what looked to be surprisingly firm biceps. She quickly absorbed tawny-colored eyes and golden-brown, sun-kissed hair, feathered perfectly across his forehead. And that tan! She'd have bet everything she owned he hadn't acquired that deep bronze tan sitting in a boardroom. She experienced a twinge of annoyance. Mr. High-

Roller probably spent more time playing than working.

She shook his hand reluctantly. His fingers were smooth and warm, while hers were dry and chapped from daily exposure to dishwater. The dishwasher had died within weeks of the day Rick had left. Money had been almost as scarce then as it was now.

Fate, Cass decided wearily, had had it in for her ever since. Even now. *Especially* now. She wore her usual summer uniform of shorts and T-shirt; she was very much afraid that if she took the time to look, she'd find the remains of Emily's lunch spattered on her shirt. She'd never felt more frazzled or unattractive in her life.

It didn't help when her son stated proudly, "You should have been here, Mom. He had the fire out in nothing flat."

Tyler slanted the boy a wry look. "I think you're sending praise in the wrong direction, young man. From what I understand, your older sister was the one who had the sense to hustle everyone outside."

Katie flushed with pleasure. Cass's gaze lingered on him for a moment. Maybe, she conceded cautiously, he wasn't so bad, after all.

Her eyes flitted to her daughter. Katie caught the silent approval in her glance and smiled. Cass's heart twisted. Katie had always been mature and level-headed; Cass often reflected it was due to growing up with three younger siblings. But Katie had had to grow up rather quickly the last two years. Her mother regretted it deeply, yet didn't know what she'd have done without Katie.

"Kate," Cass suggested softly, "why don't you take Emily into the family room and change her diaper?

Todd, will you get the box of diapers from the car and take them inside to your sister?"

Katie stepped inside and reached for Emily. She started to settle the little girl against her, then stopped abruptly. "Mom!" she cried in horror. "She's sprung a leak!"

It wasn't until then that Cass became aware of the damp spot on her own hip. Embarrassed, she flushed and glanced at their visitor, who looked just as startled as Katie. Quickly she turned back to the children and said sharply, "Todd and Katie, please do as you're told. And the rest of you come in and go watch TV while I take a look at this mess."

One by one the children filed into the house and past her. Cass heaved a weary sigh and turned her attention to the water heater.

"It looks to me," said a low voice, "like the connections on top shorted out and started the fire." Her new neighbor stepped up and pointed to the charred metal near the wall. "Unless your husband is a plumber or an electrician, it'll probably take a serviceman to repair it. You may even need a new one," he added matter-of-factly.

Wonderful, Cass thought glumly. Just wonderful. But before she had a chance to say a word, Trisha stuck her head around the corner. "Mommy doesn't have a husband," she announced. "And we don't have a daddy, because my dad—"

"Trisha!" Cass longed to clamp her hand over the child's mouth; instead she caught her arm and marched her into the hallway. "You're supposed to be in the family room with everyone else! Move it, young lady!"

Turning back and finding a pair of curious brown eyes upon her was a disconcerting sensation. Not only that, but now that she was alone with her new neighbor, her tiny utility room seemed smaller yet. Cass laid a hand upon her dryer, conscious of an unfamiliar knot in the pit of her stomach. The feeling caught her wholly off guard. Fancy pants or no, she couldn't deny Mr. High Roller—or rather, Tyler Grant—possessed an intensely masculine aura.

It was almost a relief to turn her attention to a more immediate problem. How was she supposed to explain about Rick? She certainly wasn't going to tell a perfect stranger the truth!

But he was still watching her with that faintly quizzical expression.

She tucked a long strand of hair behind her ear, knowing she looked windblown and disheveled and wondering why she even cared. "I'm divorced," she said finally. There. At least she wasn't lying.

Tyler surveyed her closely. She had paused only fractionally, but he'd glimpsed the faint shadow that had crossed her features just before she lifted her chin. He wanted to say he was sorry, yet something—a hint of defiance or maybe pride—warned him off.

He wondered once more about the eight little kids; each one looked like a Munchkin. They couldn't possibly be hers, he thought in amazement. She didn't look old enough to be the mother of a fourteen-year-old; she wasn't any taller than Katie.

His eyes traveled quickly over her, but his mind displayed a vivid recall that startled him. Her hair was caught back in a youthful ponytail. She was more cute than pretty, with wide blue eyes and a pert, uptilted nose. He liked the shorts she wore. They set off to advantage the sinewy sleekness of her legs. . . . Had they gotten that way from chasing all those kids around?

"Can I ask you something?" The question startled him. He hadn't realized he'd spoken until he heard the sound of his voice.

"Sure."

Her reply came easily enough, but Tyler thought he detected a slight stiffening in her slender shoulders. Normally he wouldn't dream of being so personal; he pacified himself by reiterating that nothing about the way he'd met his new neighbor was normal.

"I hope you don't think I'm being nosy, but . . ." Oh, hell, he might as well just get it out and be done with it. "The kids here . . . are all of them yours?"

She blinked. Tyler cursed himself. He'd embarrassed not only himself, but her, as well.

Then she smiled, a blindingly sweet smile that sent a curious jolt of pleasure through him.

"Good Lord," she exclaimed and laughed. "Do I look like a saint?"

His gaze never wavered from her face. *No*, he thought. *You look like an angel when you smile like that. And did you know that when you laugh, it sets off tiny silver lights in your eyes?*

"If they're not," he returned gravely, "then you must be."

"Not me," she denied with a chuckle. "I'll lay claim to four of them, though—Katie, Todd, Samantha and Trisha. But the other four I'm baby-sitting for the summer. I know them from school."

"School?"

"The local junior high school. I'm a teacher's aide there during the school year."

She half turned, her smile fading when her eyes alighted on the water heater. "I suppose I'd better get the power shut off to this," she said with a sigh.

"And the water."

He stepped up behind her. A long arm stretched over her and twisted a valve near the wall. The smell of soap and some light, woodsy fragrance stirred her senses. He was so close that his chest pressed against her shoulder. A lean thigh molded itself against her own. Cass caught her breath, dismayed that her awareness of this man was so acute. Tyler Grant's nearness triggered an unexpected tingling in places she shouldn't even be thinking about.

It only took a few seconds to close the water valve, but to Cass it seemed like an eternity. By the time he moved away, her chest was tight. She drew in a deep breath of air.

"I'll go turn the power off too, if you'd like."

Cass wasn't quite sure what to make of her response to this stranger, but she was suddenly anxious to be rid of him.

She shook her head. "Thanks, but I can manage. It's just a matter of flipping the circuit breaker in the garage." She smiled brightly and even offered her hand. "I really don't know how to thank you for what you did, Mr. Grant. And I apologize if we've managed to ruin your day."

You just made *my day,* a voice in Tyler's mind whispered. The thought leaped out at him before he could stop it.

"You know," he remarked softly, "I didn't catch your name."

He took her hand. Her heartbeat quickened. Did he hold her hand longer than necessary?

She moistened suddenly dry lips. "It's Cass. Cass Lawrence."

His gaze searched her face. "Will you do something for me, Cass Lawrence?"

"Sure," she said faintly.

"Will you let me know if there's anything else I can do?"

There was something warm, almost comforting in the probing of his eyes—and something that frightened her, as well.

She heard herself murmur her agreement, and felt a slight squeeze of her fingers before her hand was released. He stepped back, the tiniest of smiles curving his lips. "Good," he murmured. "I'll see you around, Cass Lawrence."

Still a little dazed, Cass watched him step out the back door. But the minute he was out of sight, reality returned with a vengeance.

She recalled the niggling dread in his eyes when he'd asked if all eight children were hers. At the time she'd thought the question was funny.

Now it made her wince.

I'll see you around, Cass Lawrence.

Sure you will, she thought grimly. No doubt Tyler Grant wouldn't be any more friendly than the Campbells. Oh, he might nod a civil hello occasionally or smile politely while picking up the mail. After all, he was Mr. High-Roller from Chicago, and she was plain old Cass Lawrence of Crystal Lake, divorced mother of four....

That alone was enough to scare any man away.

TEN O'CLOCK found Cass tucking in the kids for the night. After that she decided to crawl between the sheets of her own bed and make out her grocery list. It wasn't much of a way to soothe her frazzled nerves, but at least it kept her mind from drifting every few seconds to the disaster in her utility room.

Her mouth turned down when she flicked back the covers of her king-size bed—the bed Rick had insisted they buy. She'd always liked their cozy old double bed. This one was far too big for this modest little room, big enough for one person to get lost in...and too damned lonely.

She was in the midst of scribbling *peanut butter* at the bottom of the list when she heard a slight rustle. She looked up and saw Katie hovering in the doorway.

"Don't tell me," she said dryly. "Trish won't be quiet."

Katie shook her head; Cass thought she seemed a little anxious. "I just wanted to see if it was okay if I took a Tylenol. My teeth hurt."

Cass smiled slightly. Early this morning Katie had had her first monthly visit to the orthodontist to have her braces tightened. As he'd warned, it wasn't always a painless procedure. "Sure, honey."

Her smile drooped when her daughter traipsed down the hallway and opened the medicine cabinet. Cass had had to borrow the down payment for Katie's braces from her parents. Because of the dratted hot-water heater, tomorrow she'd have to call and see if the monthly payment they'd agreed on could wait a few weeks. Cass knew neither her mother nor father would mind, yet she hated being beholden to anyone, even to her parents.

Right now she could have cheerfully strangled her ex-husband. There was only one hitch: she didn't have the foggiest notion where he was.

Katie returned and stood in the doorway again. "Can I come in and talk for a minute, Mom?"

Cass patted the spot next to her. Katie's eyes sparkled for an instant, and she bounced on to the bed the way Trisha might have. But the next second, the lights in her eyes dimmed.

Cass put aside her pad and pencil and slipped an arm around her. "What's on your mind, hon?"

Katie sighed. "I was just wondering about the water heater, Mom. How long before it's fixed?"

Her mother chuckled. "You didn't like going back a hundred years and heating up dishwater on the stove, hmm? Your brother and sisters thought it was great fun." She ruffled Katie's wavy hair. "Count your blessings, Kate. The repairman said he'd be here tomorrow afternoon."

Katie didn't look at all reassured. "Will it cost a lot to fix, Mom?"

Cass hesitated. She'd been lucky enough to catch her insurance agent before he left his office for the weekend. He'd stopped by on his way home from work.

This time she chose her words carefully. "Our household insurance will cover most of the replacement cost..."

"But not all of it?"

Cass felt a twinge of despair. Most of the time Katie was a normal, happy-go-lucky teenager. But her daughter was also a rather wise fourteen—and very aware of their circumstances.

Cass shook her head, then spied three little faces in the doorway.

A pajama-clad Todd gazed at her dejectedly. "Gee," he muttered. "I guess that means I can't get a skateboard this summer."

Samantha poked him in the ribs. "You don't need a skateboard!"

"And you don't need a dog!"

"Todd and Sam, please don't argue!" To Cass's horror, she heard her voice crack. Four pairs of eyes swung to her at once. Suddenly the air went still.

Trisha ran across the floor and hopped onto the bed. Round blue eyes peered up at her suspiciously. "Mommy, you're not crying, are you?"

"'Course she's not!" snapped Sam. "She never cries!"

And she hadn't, not for a long, long time. But it had taken Cass buckets of tears before she'd decided once and for all that any man who'd done what Rick had wasn't worth crying over.

She'd come a long way since then. But just for an instant, time went into reverse. Memories crowded in, and a vision she couldn't shut out. She'd never forget Samantha's heart-wrenching cries that long-ago day. "Why, Mommy?" she'd sobbed. "Why did Daddy leave us? What did we do?"

Cass had sat there helplessly, holding her daughter tightly and wishing she had an answer. Every so often, Sam would ask those very same questions again.

Cass still didn't have an answer.

Bitterness choked her, but she held out her arms to Sam and Todd. "Come here," she whispered, swallowing the catch in her voice and trying with her eyes to convey her regret to both of them. She gathered all four children against her. "Someday," she whispered fiercely, "someday I'll find the money to go back to college and finish my degree."

She slipped an arm around Trisha and brought her close. "And then you'll have that pink bicycle you've wanted for so long, Trisha Lawrence. And you, young man—" she smiled shakily at Todd "—will have a brand-new shiny skateboard. Sam will have a dog to take care of, and Katie will have her stereo."

They all laughed and cuddled against her, content for the moment to share their mother's fanciful mood.

Trisha slid chubby arms around her mother's neck. "Can I sleep in here tonight?"

Cass hugged her tight. "I don't see why not."

As it happened, Katie and Samantha crawled in beside her, as well. Todd even dragged in his sleeping bag and laid it in front of the closet.

The room was crowded that night, but it was crowded with love.

3

TYLER RUBBED the back of his neck uncertainly. His wary gaze drilled into Cass Lawrence's front door. He had to be crazy. It was eight o'clock in the morning. A Saturday. He still needed to plow through the pile of corporate annual reports in his office. It was none of his business that his closest neighbor had run into a little hard luck. So what, he asked himself worriedly, was he doing here?

The doorbell echoed inside the house. His gaze flitted to the window. The drapes were still closed. Maybe they were still asleep. Maybe...

The door opened. Suddenly Tyler knew exactly why he was here.

Cass appeared rather startled right now, much the same as he'd been at her appearance yesterday. Yet he hadn't been able to forget the way she'd looked when she'd told him she was divorced. He'd sensed something inside her that was hidden from the rest of the world, something elusive and...sad.

"Hi." He gave her his friendliest smile.

Cass wanted to sink through the floor. This morning her neighbor wore crisp tan slacks and a spotless white golf shirt. She, on the other hand, was barefoot. Her attire consisted of a faded pair of denim cutoffs, and a cast-off T-shirt from her daughter that sported a happy-go-lucky dinosaur wearing a football helmet. To make matters worse, she'd been up since six, scrubbing the sooty residue from her utility room walls, and no doubt she looked it.

She winced when his gaze lingered on the silly dinosaur emblazoned on her chest. This, Cass decided sourly, was probably a first for him. Somehow she didn't think her present attire was common among his circle.

But she adopted her best lady-of-the-manor smile and tried to pretend she wasn't flabbergasted to find him on her doorstep.

"Mr. Grant. You're up early this morning. Is there something I can help you with?"

Her poise irritated Tyler for some unknown reason. Damn! he thought in annoyance. She had her hair in that darn ponytail again. He wanted to see it down, how long it was, how… He caught himself just in time. That wasn't why he was here.

"Actually, I was hoping I could help you," he said quickly. "I'm afraid I owe you an apology."

"An apology!" Cass blinked. "Whatever for?"

Some of her coolness melted visibly. It struck him that perhaps what he'd perceived as icy distance was merely cautious reserve. Tyler was inordinately pleased, without knowing quite why.

"Because it really didn't occur to me until late last night how difficult it might be for you without hot water. So I thought I'd come over and offer you and your children the use of my shower this morning."

A shower! He might have tempted her with the world on a silver platter. The idea of a nice, hot shower had never sounded better.

Although he made the offer with a smile, Cass shifted uncertainly. Behind her, the television blared with the sounds of Saturday morning cartoons. She saw his gaze flicker to the living room, where Todd, Sam and Trisha were parked in front of the set. Her new neighbor, she decided uncomfortably, might be determined to prove himself a do-gooder, but he was a reluctant knight, indeed.

She shook her head firmly. "I wouldn't dream of imposing on you like that." She thought of Ms. Sexy Brunette, and her tone grew slightly stiff as she continued. "Besides, what will your wife think if—?"

"Oh, that's not a problem." He laughed. "I'm not married, never have been. There's just me."

Which meant Ms. Sexy Brunette was . . . what? A friend? Right, Cass thought dryly. Did men nowadays have mistresses, or was that a term left over from Victorian days? *Whoa, lady.* Did she really want to speculate on exactly what kind of relationship Ms. Sexy Brunette had with Tyler Grant?

She most certainly did not, she decided, studying him closely. Why was he even bothering with her and her family? Did he feel sorry for them? The way Rick had left them had made her rather sensitive about certain things; never again would she put herself into a position where she or the kids would feel as if they weren't wanted. Nor did she want Tyler Grant or anyone else to feel responsible for them.

But how could she say that without sounding like an ungrateful snob? She felt a pinprick of guilt, knowing that was how she'd thought of Tyler Grant before they'd met. He was probably just trying to be friendly and helpful, and here she was, digging beneath the surface for something that didn't exist. She expelled a long breath in self-disgust.

"Look," she began quietly, "I have a plumber coming out this afternoon. And I know how I must have looked to you yesterday... eight kids on my hands... and a fire.... I probably came across as a totally helpless female who didn't know what to do or where to turn."

There was a faint gleam in his eyes. "The thought never crossed my mind."

"No?" Cass felt an unwilling smile edge her lips.

"Absolutely not." He moved a step closer. "But I'd say you're stalling right now."

He delivered the statement with an easy tone and a smile that made her feel all fluttery inside. He probably knew that, too.

Her denial was less emphatic than his. "I—I'm not."

"No? Do I look like the type of man who'll eat you alive? Any of you?"

He was teasing and she was weakening. And Tyler was convinced that Suzanne was right, after all. He *was* crazy. *She's got four kids,* a niggling little voice reminded him. *Count 'em, buster... four!*

"You look," Cass stated baldly, "like a man who usually gets what he wants."

He neither agreed nor disagreed. "What I want right now is for you to call the kids, grab some clean clothes and come with me. I'm even prepared to throw in breakfast, too. Provided you cook it."

Cass felt her smile widen. "Aha. I knew there was a catch."

"And you'd know why, if you'd tasted my dinner last night. So you see, the offer isn't completely altruistic."

His expression grew more serious. "Come on, Cass. Please. You'll be back in plenty of time for your plumber."

If he had insisted, if he had pressured her, she'd have refused long ago. *Please*, he'd said. The one word that stripped all thoughts of resistance.

Amazingly, she heard herself laugh. "All right. But I'll have you know I'm teaching a cooking class Monday night at the junior high school." It was one of the advantages of working for the school district; the board had been willing to let her use their facilities for a small fee, as long as she took care of the cleanup. "So," she added, "if you're interested in attending . . ."

It was his turn to laugh. "I just might surprise you, Cass Lawrence."

TYLER'S HOUSE was everything Cass remembered and more. Rustic, yet comfortable, it had everything she'd ever dreamed of—natural oak floors and woodwork, and sloping, timbered ceilings. She caught a glimpse of the cozy, floor-to-ceiling stone fireplace in the living room and suppressed a wistful sigh.

"Hey, look! Stairs!" The double doors had barely closed behind the six of them. Trisha started to race for the wide stairway off the entryway.

Cass caught her by the back of her shirt. "Oh, no, young lady. You're not here to race up and down the stairway."

"Aw, Mom! We don't have stairs like this at home!"

Samantha giggled and addressed Tyler shyly. "Mom likes this house, too. When it was for sale, she said she'd give her eyeteeth to live here."

"She did, eh?" Tyler cast an amused glance at Cass, who wanted to sink through the floor. The fact that all of them had felt that way about this house was a sore point. "After all of you have your shower or bath or whatever, I'll give you the grand tour and then we'll have breakfast."

The three youngest settled for what Cass had always called a "spit" bath—washing hands and face and ears in the half bath downstairs. When that was finished to their mother's satisfaction, and Cass had applied the prescription cream to Trisha's ankles, Tyler turned on the television in the den. The three of them plopped down before it as if this were an everyday occurrence. Katie had gone upstairs to use the shower there. Cass was all set to wait until she'd finished, when Tyler touched her arm gently.

"There's another bathroom off my room. Why don't you use the shower there?" he suggested.

A house with more than one bathroom. This was heaven indeed! But the thought of showering in his room seemed almost . . . intimate. Cass hesitated, but he'd already started to move. She had no choice but to follow.

Heaven, indeed, she thought again, once they were upstairs. It was quiet here; the chatter of the kids and the TV seemed a million miles away. Tyler opened a door and motioned her through.

Cass stepped in and glanced around. A geometrically patterned spread covered the bed—a double, not a king. Her gaze slid swiftly away, concentrating instead on the warm earth tones of the carpet and furnishings.

Tyler brushed by her. She'd never been alone in a bedroom with any man other than Rick. This was all totally innocent, but somehow that thought kept scampering through her mind.

"Bathroom's in there," he announced cheerfully. He threw open a door on the opposite wall and waved her inside. "There's plenty of towels and soap in the linen closet."

Cass muttered a thank-you. He sounded cool and totally nonchalant, the exact opposite of the way she felt.

She watched him stride across the floor. He'd reached the door when suddenly she spoke his name. "Tyler."

He turned.

To him, perhaps, all this was a small thing. But to Cass, who was determined to prove she could make it on her own, it wasn't easy accepting help from someone else.

She gestured vaguely. "I—I just wanted to say thank you. For everything you've done."

Her voice was very low. At first she thought he hadn't heard her. Then something flashed in his eyes, and Cass had the oddest sensation that Tyler Grant knew exactly how difficult and awkward she felt about accepting his generosity.

"No problem," he said softly. The door closed gently and she was left alone. She walked into the bathroom and began to strip. Pulling off her shirt, she eyed her surroundings curiously.

Tyler's bathroom was huge, almost as big as her bedroom at home. Two entire walls were covered with mirrored tile. Tall tropical plants filled every available corner. Plushly carpeted steps ascended to the tub, equipped with a Jacuzzi. It was deep and oval and a breathtaking sapphire blue, easily big enough for two adults, a thought that made her cheeks burn. There was even a skylight centered directly overhead. As if that wasn't enough, the corner shower was nearly as large; the brass-trimmed glass door wasn't frosted, but completely clear. It would hide nothing of the person within....

Cass couldn't help it. Her gaze veered to the door leading back to the bedroom. She was sorely tempted to rush over and lock it. But the kids were downstairs, she reminded herself. Besides, she was used to the girls barging in on her. And living in a household with four females had made Todd rather considerate of his own privacy, and everyone else's, as well.

As for Tyler... *Get real*, she told herself, borrowing Katie's favorite phrase. Tyler was an attractive man. But just because this room reminded her of all things blatant and sensual and uninhibited didn't mean that he thought of her that way.

No, she couldn't forget her four children were downstairs. For that very reason Cass rushed through her shower and dressed in the clean shorts and tank top she'd brought. She hurriedly ran the comb through her hair, leaving it loose around her shoulders to dry naturally.

Everyone was still in the den when she reappeared downstairs. Tyler and Katie sat on the long leather sofa, one at each end. Todd stared longingly out the window toward the lake. Samantha, sitting on the floor in front of an overstuffed chair, spotted her mother first. "Look, Mom!" she cried happily. "Mr. Grant brought his puppy inside. Her name's Missy!"

Sure enough, there was a small, black-and-white, long-haired dog stretched out between Sam and Trisha. Cass eased to her knees. "So you're Missy." She extended her hand for the puppy to sniff, then glanced up at Tyler. "What kind of dog is she? A collie?"

Tyler didn't even get a chance to answer. "She's a shelty—that's short for Shetland sheepdog." Sam's small chest swelled importantly. "She's six months old and she'll only get an inch or so bigger. Mr. Grant said they're usually pretty shy around strangers, but I think she likes me!"

Cass swallowed a pang. Sam loved animals, especially dogs. A dog had been at the top of her Christmas list. It still hurt Cass to remember how she'd had to explain that pet food wasn't the only cost to be borne; there were shots and vaccinations and visits to the veterinarian, as well. Their budget was just a little strained right now. Maybe next year... Sam had nodded bravely, but the sheen of tears in her eyes had made Cass's throat tighten achingly.

For a moment she watched Sam's hand slide lovingly over the puppy's shiny black fur. When she rose to her feet she saw that Tyler had risen, too.

"How about that tour now?"

Todd shot eagerly to his feet. "Can we go with you down by the lake?"

"I don't see why not. Let's save it for last, though."

The other two girls got up. Sam stayed where she was, cuddling Missy. She cast a pleading look at her mother. "Can I stay here with Missy?"

Cass hesitated, then glanced at Tyler. "It's okay by me," he said with a shrug.

They left the room, Katie, Trisha and Todd ahead of them. Cass paused and touched Tyler's arm. "Thanks." She flashed a grateful smile. "Sam's the big animal lover in the family. And she's been wanting a dog for ages."

"Yes," he said dryly. "I gathered that."

Their eyes met; Tyler fell silent, his expression suddenly intent. Cass experienced a flurry of self-consciousness. One hand fluttered nervously, guiding a silky strand of hair behind her ear; Cass was far too aware of the unexpected clamor of her heart thudding against her ribs.

The silence stretched out. They were so close that she could see tiny flecks of gold in his eyes. And her lips were on a level with the wild jungle of dark curls at the base of his throat.

She swallowed dryly, unable to look away. It was as if she were waiting; waiting for something to happen. . . .

"Mom! Come 'ere and have a look at this. This is the neatest-looking computer I've ever seen!"

Todd's excited cry reached her ears. Dawning comprehension washed across Tyler's features, quickly followed by a look of sheer panic. Cass wasn't sure who bolted first, she or Tyler.

She cringed at the sight that met her eyes. Perched at one end of a massive desk, Todd hovered over a computer monitor and keyboard. Trisha was at the other end, all ten fingers poised on the desk top. She peered eagerly over the top.

"Mommy, look!" she cried when Cass burst into the room. "There's an adding machine! Wouldn't this be a great place to play store? I could use this for a cash register!"

Katie stood between the two. She glanced quickly toward the two anxious adults. "It's all right, Mom," she said hastily. "I made sure they didn't touch anything."

Tyler's desperate expression relaxed. He caught Cass's look and gave her a sheepish half smile. Cass smiled weakly in return, but felt a faint tug at her heart. Her children were not destructive or unmanageable; they were, however, as active and curious as the next.

"Hey," Todd said again. "You got any games for this computer?"

Cass sent her son a look of despair, groaning inwardly.

Tyler ran a hand through his hair. "Oh, it has a ton of games," he admitted. A slow grin edged his mouth. "But I'm afraid I don't know how to play a one of them. I use it mostly for business—stock predictions and that kind of thing."

Cass had marched over and seized Trisha's hand, deciding she'd better get her daughter as far away from temptation's grasp as possible. At Tyler's declaration she sent him a quizzical glance. "You're a stockbroker?"

Tyler explained he'd worked as a trader for a number of years. "It can be pretty nerve-racking at times," he finished, "which is why I decided to bow out."

Bow out. Cass found the phrase disturbing—that was exactly what Rick had done.

"Anyway," he continued, "I'm starting a newsletter for investment firms and banking institutions. And I'll be doing a little freelance consulting occasionally."

Those words gave her pause, a great deal of it, in fact. This would be a warm, comfortable room to work in.

No doubt Tyler had had that in mind when he moved in. Her eyes lingered on the wide window behind his desk. Just beyond was the tall row of trees that separated his property from her backyard.

"So you'll be working from home?" She tried not to sound too worried.

"That's right. Believe me, it'll be a pleasure not having to worry about travel time, parking hassles and rush-hour traffic."

Cass's mind was off and running. Hmm, she thought as they left the room. And *she* would have to worry about keeping her own kids and four additional charges quiet during the week. Thank heaven, the park was only a block away.

She was beginning to wish she hadn't consented to breakfast, but Tyler insisted. She also discovered that he truly meant her to cook. Now that the time was here, she didn't feel entirely comfortable poking around in someone else's kitchen. But Tyler didn't seem to mind; he busied himself setting the table and putting out ingredients for pancakes. And when he pronounced the first bite "absolutely the best he'd ever eaten," she decided the effort was worth it.

She was glad they got through the meal with no more than the usual minor catastrophes. Todd and Katie argued over the last piece of bacon. Sam bumped her head on the table, reaching for her napkin when it dropped to the floor. Trisha knocked over her glass, but luckily she'd just drained the last of her orange juice.

He watched in amazement, though, as all four children picked up their plates and glasses when they'd finished. They each marched over to the sink, rinsed their plates and stacked them neatly on the counter.

Katie turned around. Her gaze rested shyly on Tyler. "Would you like me and Sam to start the dishes?"

His features reflected a hint of surprise, then he waved them away with a smile. "Don't bother. I'll put them in the dishwasher later."

Katie's face lighted up. The significant look she directed at her mother was half triumphant, half wistful. Cass could almost see the thought running through Katie's mind. *Gee, a dishwasher that works....*

She heaved a silent sigh. Lake frontage. Adding machines. Puppies and dishwashers. No doubt her children thought their fairy godmother—or godfather—had moved in next door.

For Cass it was a sobering thought. There was little consolation in knowing that she did the best she could. Her children had never been spoiled, but there had once been a time when they could afford little indulgences now and then. Now free spending was a thing of the past.

"Can we go back into the den and watch TV?"

"Sure," she said rather absently. "But remember we'll be leaving in a few minutes."

It wasn't until they had all filed from the room that she noticed Tyler looking at her. "I must say," he remarked, "those four aren't afraid to do their fair share."

His unexpected praise was heartwarming. "They're good kids," she said honestly, hoping she didn't sound defensive. "If they weren't, the last year and a half would have been ten times harder for me." Too late she realized what she'd said; the last thing she wanted was for Tyler to feel sorry for her.

But he said nothing. Cass lowered her lashes and rose quickly, conscious of his silent scrutiny. She moved across the room to the sink and stuck her own plate beneath the rush of water, watching the remains of her breakfast float away. If only she could wipe away the hurt and the pain that still touched their lives as easily.

Oh, she knew she put up a brave front. She had picked up the pieces of her life and forged ahead, but there were times she just couldn't forget. The knowledge that Rick had no longer wanted them—any of them—was still there, like a pebble in her shoe.

And when she turned around and faced Tyler, she had the feeling he knew, too.

For the longest time he said nothing. He watched her closely, his features reflecting a compassion she hadn't expected. But there was a strange sort of tension in the air, a tension Cass didn't want to acknowledge right now.

. She stepped forward to clear the rest of the table.

He caught her hand. "Is that how long you've been divorced? A year and a half?"

The words hung between them. She pretended not to see the silent question in his eyes. He was waiting for her to say more, she realized, but she couldn't. Her thoughts were tinged with self-mockery. She'd never quite gotten the hang of trying to explain why her husband had run off.

She tugged at her fingers; Tyler refused to let go. Yet despite the strength of his grip, there was caring in his eyes. His expression should have been reassuring; instead she found it wholly disturbing.

His fingers wrapped warm and tight about her own. Cass found herself seized, too, by an almost painful awareness. Tyler had such wonderfully masculine hands, long and strong looking. She felt herself go hot, then cold. She hadn't looked at a man, really looked at a man, since before she'd married Rick. Certainly not after.

But Tyler Grant reminded her of things better left in the past; he reminded her that she was a woman who'd known no man's touch for a long, long time.

"Is it, Cass?" His voice was low, but insistent.

Dredged up from deep within her, she found the pride that had been her saving grace these long months alone. She looked him straight in the eye. "Yes," she said clearly. "I divorced my husband eighteen months ago."

And that, Tyler noted rather grimly, was that. She'd made it abundantly clear her divorce wasn't something she cared to discuss. Was she carrying a torch for her ex? The notion disturbed him.

For an instant Cass thought he meant to relinquish her hand. Instead, his grip only tightened.

"I have the feeling," he said very quietly, "you're a very direct woman, Cass Lawrence."

A pang swept through her. She tried to be, yes. Maybe it was because Rick had been such a coward. He hadn't been able to look her in the eye and tell her he wanted out. Instead he had sneaked away like a thief in the night.

Trisha raced into the kitchen. "Can we go now, Mom? You said we could make play dough this morning."

Cass was never more grateful for the presence of her small daughter. She snatched her hand away from Tyler and turned to Trisha.

Behind her, Tyler got to his feet. "You *make* play dough?" he echoed. "I was under the impression it came from the toy store."

"Oh, ours is lots better." Trisha beamed up at him. "Mommy uses flour and salt and food coloring. She makes lots of other things, too. My grandpa says she makes the best raspberry jelly he ever tasted—and she takes the seeds out, too. And she makes cinnamon applesauce and tomato juice...."

A thick chestnut eyebrow rose. "Does she now," Tyler murmured. "Seems to me your mother is a very talented woman." His eyes returned to Cass. "And she's pretty, too."

Right, Cass scoffed inwardly. She didn't believe him for a minute, and it wasn't only because of the thread of laughter lurking in his voice. She had a pretty darn good idea of the kind of woman a man like Tyler Grant favored—a sleek sophisticate like Ms. Sexy Brunette. No, a mother with four kids would never measure up for a man like Tyler Grant.

She stepped forward briskly. "Trish, go get your brother and sisters and tell them it's time to go. We've bothered Tyler long enough."

"Now wait just a minute—"

But Cass didn't stop to listen. She was just a step behind Trisha, gathering her children around her and playing mother hen, a role she was entirely comfortable with. She was just a little off balance with Tyler Grant and was suddenly anxious to be in her own home, in her own kitchen, where she was confident and sure of herself.

That thought stayed with her while she politely thanked Tyler, bade him goodbye and herded the kids home.

Katie dropped back beside her.

"He likes you, Mom. He likes you a lot." Her eyes gleamed. "Did you notice?"

Cass couldn't believe she'd heard right. *"What?"*

"He does, Mom! I saw the way he was looking at you. Like . . ."

Cass laid her hand on the front door. "Like what?" she demanded. Todd, Trisha and Sam had gone around to the backyard. She opened the door and motioned her daughter inside.

"You know." Katie's cheeks grew pink. "The way a man looks at a woman when he . . . well, you know. When he's *interested* in her, like . . . like Adam and Eve. Romeo and Juliet—"

"Katie!" To her horror, Cass felt a rare blush stealing into her cheeks. "Sweetie, you're talking about your *mother!* And maybe I'd better not let you watch those daytime soaps anymore!"

"Oh, come on, Mom. I'm fourteen. We had this talk a long time ago, remember?" Katie followed her mother into the kitchen. "I'm *supposed* to know these things."

Cass began tidying up automatically; the salt and pepper still on the table, putting away yesterday's mail, the cereal box on the counter.

"Katie," she said after a moment. "You're imagining things. Tyler was just being nice."

"I don't think so." She turned around in time to see a mysterious smile flit across her daughter's face. "I don't think so at all."

Cass felt her heart slam into fifth gear. It wasn't true, she told herself staunchly. Katie was mistaken. Tyler couldn't have looked at her the way Katie said . . . or could he?

She drew a deep, unsteady breath. She was not a woman given to flights of fancy. She was far too practical to ignore the tiny voice inside that told her she could get lost in a world that was far beyond her reach.

Just for an instant her mind ran wild. She liked Tyler Grant. And yes, she found him immensely attractive. No doubt he knew exactly how to make a woman *feel* like a woman again....

Katie picked an apple from the bowl on the table and started from the room. "By the way," she said lightly, "you might want to take the box of Cheerios out of the fridge, Mom. No one will ever find it there."

Cass toppled from the heights; it was an eye-opening trip back to earth.

She knew her smile was rueful as she stowed the Cheerios in their rightful place in the pantry. No, now was definitely not the time to become a dreamer. And the idea of Cass Lawrence, mother of four, together with a man like Tyler Grant... That was more than just a dream.

It was an outright fantasy.

4

"Mom?"

"Yes, Todd." Stationed near the stove, busily butter-
ing bread for toasted cheese sandwiches, Cass spoke
absently. She didn't bother to turn around.

"Can I go over to Tyler's tonight?"

Tyler. The name succeeded in grabbing her attention as nothing else could have. They hadn't spoken to
him since Saturday, though she'd seen him yesterday
talking to one of the other neighbors. Knife in hand, she
turned and faced her son. "Why?" she asked, frown-
ing.

"I saw him walking his dog this morning. He told me
I could come over some evening and we'd see if we
could figure out how to play some of his computer
games."

Cass sighed. Todd looked so anxious, she couldn't
bear to tell him Tyler was only being nice. She couldn't
stop the flicker of irritation that shot through her. She
wished Tyler wouldn't get Todd's hopes up by making
promises he didn't intend to keep. The kids did without so much already; they never complained because
they weren't able to buy the latest trendy items like so
many of their friends. Still, there was another possi-
bility that troubled her.

"Todd," she said slowly, "I'm really not sure you
should be calling Tyler by his first name. In fact, you

really should call him Mr. Grant. Secondly, I hope you didn't ask him about those games, or drop any big hints that . . ."

Todd's head drooped. "Maybe I did drop a hint or two," he mumbled. The next instant his head came up. "But he told me to call him Tyler—and he did tell me to drop over sometime. So can I go over there tonight? Please?"

She hesitated. "Todd," she said gently. "Tyler is a very busy man. And I have the cooking class at school tonight, remember?" She winced when Todd's face fell. "Besides, maybe you should give Tyler a few weeks to get settled in. Okay?"

Todd didn't have a chance to agree or disagree. Brian and Dave filed into the kitchen. "Who's Tyler?" Brian asked, glancing from Cass to Todd.

Todd shoved his hands into the pockets of his jeans. "The man who moved into the Campbell place."

"Oh, yeah. The guy with the computer that has dozens of video games." Todd had apparently been doing a little heavy-duty bragging of his own. Brian's snicker made it clear he was rather skeptical of Todd's claim.

Cass heaved a silent sigh. Eight-year-old Dave was shy and thoughtful, like his sister Sara, who was a year younger. They were quiet and well mannered; Cass didn't think she could have handled four children besides her own if Sara and Dave hadn't been such good kids. But Brian, an only child, was used to getting his own way. He was sometimes boastful, occasionally a little stubborn and challenging. He liked to be one up on everyone else and usually made no secret of it. Most of the time the three boys got along fine, but every so often Brian and Todd clashed.

This was one of those times. Todd was prickling visibly. "You don't believe me? He uses it for..." Cass could almost see him fumbling around in his limited vocabulary. His eyes flashed when he found the word he wanted. "He uses it for business!"

"Business?" Brian snickered again and slid into the chair behind the table. "He's home all the time! I bet he doesn't even have a job."

"He does, too! He's got an office in his house, and that's where he has his computer."

"Aw, come on. I never heard of anybody working at home! My dad drives all the way to Milwaukee to go to work."

"Well, Tyler doesn't have to, 'cause he works at home." Todd's chin rose. "If you don't believe me, just ask my mom!"

Three pair of eyes turned expectantly to Cass. She smiled at Brian. "Todd's right, Brian. Mr. Grant does work at home, which is why I asked all of you to keep the noise down to a dull roar, especially when you're outside."

"Oh." Brian looked embarrassed. It was Dave who asked curiously, "What's he do?"

Todd dropped onto the chair next to Dave. "He's in finance."

His tone was so self-important, Cass smothered a laugh. Dave looked as doubtful as Brian had just seconds earlier. "What's that?" he asked.

Todd bit his lip. "I dunno," he muttered. "Something to do with banks."

Cass decided to come to his rescue. "That it does," she told the three boys. "But it also has to do with money. How to spend it, how to save it—"

"How to make it?"

She turned back to the stove. "That, too. I suppose if you wanted to know what to do with your money, or how to make more with what you already have, you'd go to someone like Tyler. From what I understand, he's a little like an adviser."

She laid the sandwiches upon the grill with brisk efficiency. "Do me a favor, son. Go tell the girls to get washed up. Lunch is almost ready."

IN TYPICAL KID FASHION, Todd and Brian were again the best of buddies throughout the rest of the day. Cass had just begun to breathe more easily, but then Emily's mother had a flat tire on the way home from work and was late picking her up. In order to get to her class on time, Cass was forced to leave the dinner dishes heaped on the counter.

About fifteen children had signed up for the class, and several were waiting outside when she arrived. She hurriedly unlocked the doors and led the way into the home economics kitchen. Katie had offered to help with the preparations, and Todd was left in charge of Samantha and Trisha. They wasted no time, charging back outside to the playground.

Between the sultry air of the warm summer evening and hurrying to get everything set out before class time, Cass was left feeling just a little frazzled. She and Katie and one of the mothers who'd stayed got everyone registered, and she was pleased to note there were many familiar faces. Several boys had showed up, as well.

Finally she stepped to the front of the classroom. "Okay, let's get started," she announced, looking at the sea of faces before her. "I thought breakfast would be the logical place to begin, so we'll be learning how to prepare the basics—bacon, eggs, pancakes—and French toast if there's time."

One of the boys groaned. "I don't even eat breakfast," he grumbled.

"But you should," Cass said with a chuckle. "And you're about to find out why, too. Besides, wouldn't your mother just love it if you surprised her with breakfast in bed, a breakfast you cooked all by yourself?" She laughed. "I know I would. Breakfast in bed would be heaven!"

The boy gave her a sheepish grin.

She touched briefly on nutrition, then began her demonstration at the long counter in the front of the room. Afterward, she separated the children into groups and sent them to the workstations for some hands-on experience.

It was while the groups were dispersed that she heard several loud giggles from several girls of Katie's age. "Ladies," she reproved them absently, busy rinsing a mixing bowl in the sink. "This is not a gab session. If you waste time talking, you won't have time to eat what you've prepared—which might not be any great loss if you haven't been paying attention."

She turned off the water and pushed a stray hair from her cheek with the back of her hand, then glanced over at them. They were staring at the door in the rear of the room. With a frown she followed the direction of their gaze.

She scarcely heard the low masculine chuckle. All she registered were golden-brown eyes twinkling back at her, a long male body lounging against the wall, and a crooked half smile she was sure was designed expressly to make the feminine heart skip a beat.... And hers was no exception.

Tyler Grant. What was he doing here? When he'd said he couldn't cook, she remembered kidding him about being interested in this class. What was it he'd said? *I just might surprise you, Cass Lawrence.*

She was immensely grateful for the swarm of activity around her when he advanced into the room.

"How long have you been here?" she managed to whisper.

"Long enough to discover that you think breakfast in bed would be heaven." His smile deepened. "Surprised you, huh?"

"I'll say." The confession slipped out before she could stop it. She shifted uneasily, a little angry at herself and wondering what it was about him that made her feel like a gauche teenager.

It was a question, she concluded glumly, that was utterly ridiculous. Tyler Grant was smooth, sophisticated and worldly...everything she wasn't.

She attempted a smile. "I—I need to get back to the kids."

"You don't mind if I watch, do you? I could certainly use a few lessons when it comes to the kitchen."

"Of course not." Secretly she doubted he needed lessons in anything. Tyler Grant struck her as an intensely capable man who knew his way around the boardroom...and the bedroom, as well, if Ms. Sexy Brunette was any indication.

Cass didn't know how she got through the rest of the class. She supervised while the kids poured and mixed, giving instructions here, nodding approval there. All the while she tried her best to ignore Tyler's presence.

She failed miserably.

The minute the class was dismissed, Todd ran from where he and his sisters had been sitting for the last ten minutes. "Mom! How come Tyler's here?"

"Because Tyler is about to starve to death if he eats one more frozen dinner," interjected a deep male voice from behind her.

"I like 'em," Todd announced. "But Mom won't buy them 'cause she says they have too much fat."

Samantha peeked shyly up at Tyler. "My mom knows a lot about what we should and shouldn't eat. She was going to be a . . ." Her brow furrowed as she struggled to find the right word.

"A nutritionist," Katie supplied.

"Really?" Tyler tipped his head to the side and regarded Cass. "What stopped you?"

Cass opened her mouth, but once again she didn't get to say a word. Between Tyler and her four children, it seemed the art of speech was unnecessary.

Todd answered for her again. "She quit college and got married. To my dad," he clarified unnecessarily.

"But someday she's gonna go back." Trisha planted herself right in front of her new friend. "And then I get to have a new bike instead of Sam's old one. And Todd gets a skateboard, and Sam gets to have her very own dog. And Katie's gonna have a stereo for her room."

Her tone was so earnestly certain that Cass felt a dozen different emotions squeeze into her heart. Anger. Despair. A feeling of helplessness. Trisha, in the way of children, possessed such blind faith in her mother. She never questioned; she simply believed. Was it wrong to let her believe in something that might never happen?

In the small silence that followed, Cass became aware of Tyler's gaze lingering on her profile. His speculative expression made her cringe. She couldn't chastise the kids for something they didn't understand. But she didn't want Tyler, or anyone else, feeling sorry for them.

The laugh she uttered was a trifle forced, she knew. "You mean I actually get to say something? Maybe I'd better while I still have the chance." She glanced at Tyler. "I hope you weren't disappointed with the class."

He shook his head. "Not at all," he assured her.

And he wasn't lying. He'd just learned far more than he had bargained for, and realized he'd been remarkably obtuse not to have made the connection before now. Cass's job as a teacher's aide only lasted nine months out of the year. Todd had told him yesterday that she also baby-sat after school; no doubt she was baby-sitting this summer to make up for the loss in income.

He was also reminded of what Trisha had said the day they'd met. *Mommy doesn't have a husband. And we don't have a daddy, because my dad . . .* Cass had cut her off, and he hadn't given it a second thought. But he hadn't mistaken the fleeting look of pain that passed over her features just now. Did it have something to do with her ex-husband?

Tyler didn't want to think so. Damn, but he didn't. But he was just as determined to find out what was behind that look of pain, and the very fierceness of his conviction surprised him.

He felt her gaze on him while he helped her and Katie straighten the kitchen. When she reached for the box of supplies she'd brought in, his hands were there before hers, and he told her firmly he would carry it out to her car. She argued it wasn't necessary; he didn't bother insisting, but simply turned and asked Samantha to run ahead and hold the door open for him.

When they had finished stowing everything in the back of her car, he saw Todd gesture at the sleek, silver-painted foreign sports car parked next to the family's battered station wagon. Shining eyes looked up at Tyler. "Gee," the boy breathed. "Is this car yours?"

Tyler nodded. There was no mistaking the longing on the boy's face. "How'd you like to ride home with me?" he asked after a moment. "As long as it's okay with your mom." He glanced at Cass.

"Sure, honey," Cass said. She couldn't blame Todd for wanting to ride in Tyler's car. In fact, she was sorely tempted to laugh. Beauty and the beast, she thought as her gaze bounced between the two vehicles. Samantha had dented the front fender before she discovered her bike actually came equipped with brakes; then Cass had been sideswiped sitting at a stoplight several months ago, and the list didn't end there. She often thought her ten-year-old station wagon had more battle scars than a Sherman tank could ever have had.

The minute they were home again, Todd raced over, his face bright and excited. "Boy, Mom, you should see the inside of Tyler's car! There's a million dials and gadgets."

Cass's eyes flickered to Tyler, who had followed at a more sedate pace. Clearly rather embarrassed by the boy's enthusiasm, he shrugged it off and planted himself squarely next to her, once again reaching for the box of supplies. He pulled back and eased the box a little higher in his arms, chuckling when he heard her sigh in sheer exasperation. She didn't argue with him this time, but wondered why he was still hanging around.

Tyler hadn't quite figured that out yet, either.

He let his eyes drift over the smooth curve of her cheek, the spray of dark lashes as she opened the door and pointed him toward the garage. Tyler trailed behind her, liking the way her hair skimmed her shoulders as she walked.

Todd had told him in the car she was thirty-four. Did one call a thirty-four-year-old woman cute? Yet Cass wasn't so much cute as fresh and natural and open. She was certainly very *different* from the other women who had passed in and out of his life the past ten years.... And there was the key word, he suddenly realized. *Different*.

Cass watched as he deposited the box on the workbench in the garage. Too late she wished she hadn't led him through the kitchen. When he stepped back inside, his gaze alighted upon the humongous stack of dishes on the counter. He didn't say a word. But then, he didn't need to. The way his eyes widened said it all. "We were running a little late when we left," Cass said lamely. Until this moment, she had forgotten she hadn't gotten around to the lunch dishes, either.

His lips twitched. "I realize the kitchen is hardly my area of expertise—" his gaze dropped to a point adjacent to her left hip "—but isn't that a dishwasher?"

"It might as well *not* be, for all the good it does," she told him lightly.

"It doesn't work?"

"No. My dad took a look at it, but it needs a lot more than a Band-Aid to fix it." Her tone was cheerful and matter-of-fact; he wondered if she realized the faint wistfulness in her expression gave her away.

If Tyler was taken aback, it was no wonder. She had eight kids here during the day and no dishwasher. Suzanne would have pulled her hair out. To her a dishwasher was as indispensable as her manicurist. Then again, the mere mention of eight kids would have sent Suzanne running all the way to China with a jet stream in her wake.

He didn't ask why Cass didn't call a plumber. Her situation was becoming clearer by the minute. Instead he gave her his most charming smile and asked where she kept the dish towels.

Cass gaped at him.

Heavy brows rose inquiringly. "You'd rather dry? Fine, then. I'll wash." He stepped up to the sink and reached for the dish soap.

Cass stared, unable to believe her eyes. Tyler Grant, Mr. High-Roller from Chicago, was standing in her kitchen with a bottle of pink dish soap in his hands. After the dose of her family he'd been given Saturday morning and again tonight, she was surprised he hadn't run the other way, clear back to Chicago!

"Tyler." She had to raise her voice in order to make herself heard. "This really isn't necessary. Katie and I can wash these. Besides, we—we really don't know each other all that well. You certainly shouldn't feel obligated to help me. You should be at home, doing whatever it is you stockbroker types do to relax. Why aren't you out playing golf or something?"

Tyler found her statement odd, because he'd just made a rather fascinating discovery. Strange as it sounded, he felt altogether comfortable with this woman. That wasn't quite the case with her four children, he found himself admitting, but maybe that was because he'd never really been around small children.

His tone was gently chiding. "In case you hadn't noticed, it's almost dark, certainly too dark to play golf. Secondly, I am most definitely not a golfer. Thirdly, there is someone before you who is ready, willing and able, so why not just leave it at that? And lastly—" his voice dropped to a husky pitch "—I'd be a fool to complain about washing dishes when I have a view as easy on the eye as you."

Cass caught her breath when his eyes made a slow, languid journey down to her feet and back up again. Her heart began to pound. There was something warm, something exciting—and yes, even flattering in the dark brown velvet of his eyes. But he couldn't possibly be serious. After all, no man in his right mind would make a play for a divorcée with four kids, especially not a man like Tyler Grant. She stifled a sound that would have been half laugh, half groan, had she let it escape.

She hadn't realized she had backed away until she heard a low chuckle.

"Hey, I'm harmless, really."

Cass found herself starting to smile. Tyler Grant harmless? In a straitjacket, perhaps. Or marooned on a desert island. . . .

"Right," she said dryly. "Just remember my mother warned me not to take candy from strangers."

"Mom!" Katie bounced into the kitchen. "Do you want me to help with the—?" She stopped short when she saw Tyler at the sink, up to the elbows in sudsy dishwater.

Tyler glanced over his shoulder. "There's no need," he said smoothly. His eyes slid back to Cass. "Your mother and I have things well under control."

He saw Katie hesitate, then look at Cass for approval. Her mother gave her a slight smile. "No dishes tonight, sweetie. But would you mind getting Samantha and Trish ready for their bath?"

"Sure thing, Mom." Katie looked as if she'd just received a gift from heaven.

Cass pulled a dish towel from the drawer. "That's the second time she's gotten out of dishes, thanks to you," she told Tyler. The lack of heat in her voice took the sting from the words. "She's going to think you're the angel on her shoulder."

"Then maybe she'll put in a good word for me with her mother."

She couldn't help but duplicate his smile. "I think," she said lightly, "someone already has."

Between the two of them, they had the dishes polished off in no time at all. Tyler didn't linger, and as Cass walked him to the door, she admitted to a niggling feeling of disappointment that he was leaving so soon. Katie was just herding Samantha and Trisha down the hall to the bath, so Cass felt free to step outside with him.

The summer night was still and heavy and warm. A faint breeze curled around their figures, bringing with it the spicy scent of after-shave.

She stretched out a hand, only to let it drop back to her side. "I appreciate you helping with the dishes—and loading and unloading all my supplies." Her laugh was strangely breathless. "It seems I'm always thanking you—"

His fingers on her lips stifled whatever else she might have said. He shook his head, the movement almost imperceptible. His eyes never wavered from hers. "It wasn't a big deal. And I didn't mind, honestly." He smiled slightly. "Besides, it sure beats spending the evening alone."

Innocuous as she knew it was, his statement kindled a poignant ache deep inside her. There was one very big difference between them, she suddenly realized. No doubt Tyler didn't have to spend the evening alone. She had the feeling Ms. Sexy Brunette wouldn't have hesitated to heed his call. But for Cass it was a different story altogether. He had just unwittingly reminded her of how alone she was . . . and just how long it had been since she'd been touched . . . and loved.

"Right," she said, forcing a smile. "For someone like you, tonight was probably as exciting as watching grass grow."

"Well," he said with a grin. "I'll admit my mind wasn't on French toast and pancakes *all* the time." A wicked glint appeared in his eyes. "Would you like to come home with me and see my etchings?"

The thought that Tyler was even remotely serious just didn't bear thinking about. "I doubt I'm your type," she said unthinkingly.

He folded his arms across his chest and fixed her with a mock glare. "And what exactly is my type?"

"Oh, I don't know. Someone like the sexy brunette who was here last week." Cass had said the first thing that popped into her head, then wished she'd kept silent.

She had startled him, she realized. She saw it in the way his eyes flickered. But then he smiled, a slowly growing smile that held her momentarily fascinated.

"Don't be so sure about that," he drawled. "In fact, I think I'm growing rather partial to honey-colored blondes with the cutest freckles I've seen in a long, long time."

She wrinkled her nose at him. "I'd never have pegged you for a tease."

He reached out and caught not one, but both of her hands. "Neither would I." Gently he tugged her closer. Despite the amusement she saw dancing in his eyes, there was something low and intimate in his tone that sent tingly feathers of sensation fluttering down her spine.

All at once Cass wasn't certain he was teasing, after all. There had once been a time when she wouldn't have thought twice about such banter. She'd have loved it— reveled in it and joined in with no hesitation at all. But Rick's departure had left its mark. Now she only felt awkward and confused.

She saw Tyler's smile fade. Their eyes met and held endlessly. Cass was the first to look away. "I'd better get back inside," she muttered.

But his grip on her hands tightened, just enough to remind her she wasn't free. "I'm sorry, Cass." His voice was low and rough. "I upset you. I didn't mean to, I swear."

Her lips were quivering so that she could barely smile. She could scarcely speak for the hot ache that filled her throat. "It's all right," she whispered, despising the catch in her voice, despising her stupid, silly reaction to something so trivial.

But it wasn't all right. His heart wrenched at the tiny break in her voice. Tyler knew he'd said something wrong, something that reminded her of her ex-husband. He didn't know how he knew, he just did. Was she carrying a torch for him yet? All of a sudden he wanted very desperately to know, and there was one surefire way to test the theory.... He wanted to kiss her, he realized. He wanted to kiss her and drive away that look of hurt confusion.... Who was he trying to kid?

He wanted to kiss her, and he sure as hell didn't need a reason.

"Cass," he whispered. He watched her gaze trickle slowly, inevitably, to him. He held himself very still for the space of a heartbeat, then began to lower his head.

Cass felt herself tremble. What would it be like, she wondered, to have a man like Tyler Grant kiss her? Would his touch be sweet and tender? Sure and demanding? She stared into eyes as warm and potent as whiskey. Once again, just the way it had been last Saturday morning at Tyler's, she felt as if they were both waiting for something to happen....

Something did.

The screen door burst open. Two small bodies hurtled through the doorway.

"Mommy, I want to take a bath so we can play!"

"We always take a bath. I want a shower!"

"And Katie told us both to go dunk our heads in the lake!"

The two adults jerked apart almost guiltily. Cass heard a low, hissing gasp and realized it came not from her throat, but his. She bent instinctively and gathered Trisha and Samantha close to her. Summoning a dignity she hadn't known she possessed, she straightened and glanced up at Tyler.

"Duty calls," she said with a laugh that sounded oddly strangled. She'd have turned, but a hand on her arm stopped her.

"Wait," he said suddenly. "Why don't you get the kids to bed and come over to my place for a while?"

"Why?" she asked in that point-blank manner he was coming to associate with her.

"Because I think you could use a little R and R. I know for a fact you've had a long day." That was only half the truth. The other half was that Tyler had no objection to getting to know his new neighbor better—much better.

And indeed Cass was tempted, far more tempted than she cared to admit. But she shook her head. "I couldn't leave the kids alone," she said firmly.

"I'll stay up till you get back, Mom. And I'll put these two to bed as soon as they're finished with their bath," announced a cheery, matter-of-fact voice. "And Todd, too. I've done it before, remember? When you've had PTA meetings."

Katie had appeared in the doorway. She crooked her finger at Samantha and Trisha. "Come on, you two. The tub's all ready."

Cass could have cheerfully strangled her eldest daughter. Tyler Grant, sweet though he was—charming though he was—was one dangerous male...and for one very good reason.

He made her feel very female, extremely conscious of her womanhood. It had been a long, long time since she'd felt that way, Cass reluctantly acknowledged. So long that she wasn't sure she was entirely comfortable with the sensation.

He was looking at her expectantly. "That settles it, then," he murmured. "Katie is a godsend, isn't she?"

At that moment Cass wasn't so sure. But there was no way she could refuse without sounding petty. And if the truth were known, whispered a little voice inside, she didn't want to.

Neither one said anything on the short walk to his place. As they mounted the porch steps, Tyler looked at her. "Why don't we sit out here where it's cooler?" he suggested. "Besides," he added dryly, "maybe you won't feel you've deserted the home front as long as your house is in sight."

Cass glanced at him sharply. Was he making fun of her? She relaxed when she saw his eyes were filled with a teasing light.

She wrinkled her nose at him. "You sure this isn't a ploy to lure me inside to see those etchings you mentioned earlier?"

His smile was utterly disarming. "Looks like you're about to find out, doesn't it?"

Warm fingers curled around her arm. Cass felt a tiny little shiver race through her as he guided her toward a chaise lounge at the far end of the porch. Seconds later two strong hands on her shoulders eased her gently down toward the cushions. "Just sit tight," he commanded, "while I go inside for some iced tea."

Cass started to rise instinctively. "Let me help—"

She found herself propelled downward once more. "Oh, no," he countered with a shake of his head. "You're not lifting another finger tonight. You're going to sit here and enjoy doing absolutely nothing." She gasped when he swung her feet up to the cushions. He then proceeded to pull off her slip-on shoes. He straightened, hands on hips. Through the darkness, she caught the flash of a smile as he glanced down at her. It was almost as if he dared her to argue with him.

Speechless, but only for an instant, Cass decided he looked rather pleased with himself. She tucked her feet beneath her and frowned up at him. "Not only are you a tease," she accused him good-naturedly, "you're also rather bossy."

"Bossy," he repeated, then raised his brows. "A trait you're familiar with?"

"I guess I am, at that," she admitted with a rueful grin. "That's what happens when you're surrounded by kids most of the time, like I am."

"All the more reason to take a little time for yourself, once in a while."

With that he turned and headed into the house. Cass, unsure what to make of his remark, leaned back and crossed her bare feet at the ankles. She might as well do what Tyler had said—relax and enjoy the rare chance to do nothing for a change.

Inside the house, the living room was flooded with light, casting a hazy glow onto the porch. The front door opened and Tyler reappeared, carrying two tall, frosty glasses. She murmured her thanks as he handed one to her. Cass watched as he scooted a chair around at right angles to her chaise lounge.

She eyed him over the rim of her glass. "Can I ask you something?"

"Shoot."

"How did you manage to settle here in Crystal Lake? Do you have family here?"

He shook his head. "I told the realtor what I was looking for—something quiet and away from the city, without being too remote. He came up with this and the rest, as the saying goes, is history."

"But you do have family somewhere?"

He chuckled. "*Somewhere* just about sums it up. My parents have a condo on Lake Shore Drive, but they only spend a few months a year there. They've developed a migratory nature since my father retired, I'm afraid. They fly south to Arizona in the winter. Summers are usually spent at their house in Michigan's upper peninsula."

"So your father's retired." She eyed him curiously. "Was he in finance, too?"

"My father isn't the gambler I am," he said with a laugh. "He was in advertising."

"I'll bet you're an only child." It slipped out before she could stop it. She hoped the words didn't sound like an accusation.

"That obvious, huh?"

His tone made her smile. "Actually, yes," she admitted. "It's just that you seemed a little overwhelmed the day we met and . . ." Her voice trailed away.

"You have to admit," he commented wryly, "that coming into a house with eight small children is enough to overwhelm anyone."

And four were enough to make most men run in the opposite direction. It was a wonder he hadn't freaked, she thought with a silent groan. Or maybe it was just a matter of time. . . . There was an odd little stab in the region of her heart.

"True," she agreed, feeling her smile waver.

He tipped his head to the side and regarded her quizzically. "Does that put me on your hit list?"

Cass was relieved to see he was teasing. "Of course not. But you're not what I thought," she said.

His eyes were twinkling. "This promises to be interesting. Exactly what did you think I'd be like?"

"When I found out you were some kind of mover and shaker from Chicago, I figured you'd be a real stuffed shirt. Boring and pompous and—"

"And looking down my nose at you from my ivory tower?"

Too late, Cass realized he might think she was taking potshots at him. "But you're not like that at all," she assured him hastily. "In fact, you're really very nice," she ended lamely.

Nice. Suddenly Tyler wasn't quite so amused. Coming from her, he found the word less than satisfactory. Well, he *had* asked, he reminded himself.

"I see," he said lightly. "Does that mean I have your approval?"

She was silent for a moment, tilting her head and regarding him with a slight smile on her lips. It was a smile that seemed to reach clear inside him.

"Yes," she said softly. "I guess it does." Before she could think better of it, she reached out and squeezed his free hand. "Welcome to the neighborhood, Tyler Grant."

The time sped by. Cass was amazed how comfortable she felt with Tyler, considering the differences in their backgrounds. And especially since they had known each other only a few days.

She jumped up with a little cry when her gaze happened to slip to Tyler's watch. It was almost midnight.

"Oh, no!" she groaned. "This time I *really* have to go."
Her anxious gaze slid to her house. The light still blazed
in the living room. She pictured Katie sprawled on the
sofa, fast asleep.

Tyler stood. "I'll walk you home."

Moments later they stood on her doorstep for the
second time. Also for the second time that night, Tyler
found himself seized by a compulsion to drag her into
his arms and smother those raspberry-colored lips with
his own.

The air grew still and close and heated. Neither one
moved; neither one said a word.

It was Cass who broke the silence. "Good night, Tyler."

To her horror, there was a slight quaver in her voice.
Was she disappointed because he made no move to kiss
her? Surely not. She and Tyler would never suit. Besides, the last thing she wanted was to be a substitute
for Ms. Sexy Brunette. But she hadn't realized until now
just how starved she was for a little adult companion-
ship . . . especially the male variety.

Tyler skimmed the curve of her cheek with his fingertips, and Cass was suddenly aware of the frantic
clamor of her heart. It was all she could do not to press
her cheek into the warm roughness of his palm.

Willpower alone made her step back. "Good night,"
she said again. She slipped inside before she could make
a total fool of herself.

Tyler was left staring at the closed door, his thoughts
a mixture of frustrated longing. He wondered if she
knew how much he'd ached to drag her into his arms.
But he'd sensed she didn't want that from him, just as
he still sensed she was just as confused as he was.

Finally he turned and started down the walk toward his house. They hadn't seen the last of each other, he promised himself adamantly. Yet even as the vow echoed through his mind, Tyler was at a total loss to explain his unexpected resolve. He had come here to live his own life, not to get involved in someone else's.

Cass had been right, he told himself staunchly. Suzanne's charms had worn thin long ago. But a woman like Cass Lawrence really wasn't his type, either.

And she had four kids, four boisterous, fun-loving kids. The very thought was enough to make him break into a cold sweat.

All at once he recalled Suzanne's parting shot. *You'll be back in Chicago by the end of the summer, at the latest.* He hated to think Suzanne might be right.

He'd never be able to stand her gloating.

5

WHEN TYLER'S DOORBELL rang the following evening, he didn't waste a second jumping up from his desk. He had no doubts about who was at the door. A pair of impossibly wide blue eyes, soft, honey-colored hair, and lips the color of raspberries flashed into his mind.

Tyler loved raspberries.

He'd been going certifiably insane the last twenty-four hours, knowing he had come so close to kissing those raspberry-colored lips, wondering what he had missed...and knowing whatever it was, it would have been unbearably sweet.

He flung open the front door, his best, welcoming smile on his lips.

Three pairs of round blue eyes peered up at him. Tyler tried hard not to let his disappointment show; he wasn't sure he succeeded.

"Hi." Todd stepped forward. "If you're not busy, could we talk to you for a minute? We need some advice. Real bad."

"Yeah," Trisha echoed soulfully. "Real bad."

Tyler glanced at Samantha, who silently echoed the pleas of her brother and sister. He felt a smile creep along his lips. It was hard to stop it from blossoming into a full-blown laugh. Judging from the earnest expressions on the three faces before him, they'd come here on a matter of life or death.

"Well," he said gravely, "this sounds serious." He closed the screen and eased himself down onto the top step of the porch. Todd planted himself next to him, while Trisha and Samantha huddled on the step in front.

Todd wasted no time in getting down to business. "Mom said you know a lot about money."

Tyler didn't know what he'd expected, but this definitely wasn't it. "Well," he said doubtfully, "that depends what you want to know."

"Mom said if a person wanted to know how to make money—and how to save it—it would be a good idea to come to someone like you."

He blinked. "That's why you're here?"

Todd nodded. "Mom said you're kind of like an adviser. So me and Sam decided the best thing we could do was come to you."

Tyler was finding it increasingly hard to keep a straight face. "A wise choice," he murmured.

Todd frowned. "We know we gotta save our money," he said glumly. "But first we gotta earn it."

Comprehension dawned in a flash. "I see," he said with a twitch of his lips. "This is so you can buy that skateboard?"

Todd nodded. Trisha jumped up. "I want a bike! The pink one in the store window!"

Tyler smiled. His gaze slid to Samantha. "And you want a dog, right?"

It was Samantha's turn to nod. "I'd give anything to have a dog like Missy," she murmured.

Tyler's eyes softened. "That reminds me." He got up and opened the front door. "Missy, come!" The dog bounded onto the porch. Samantha's eyes lighted up like a tree at Christmas when Missy yipped and danced around before her.

"She likes you," he observed with a smile.

The little girl rubbed her chin against the top of Missy's head, her face glowing. "Not as much as I like her."

Tyler caught sight of Todd's expression. The boy looked so disgruntled that he nearly lost his battle not to laugh. Tyler resumed his seat at the top of the porch steps and cleared his throat. "Now then. Where were we?"

"We thought maybe you could help us figure out what kind of work the three of us could do to earn some money."

"Katie baby-sits for the Reeds and the McKinleys," Sam said mournfully. "But I'm not old enough to baby-sit."

"Yeah," muttered Todd. "And she gets an allowance for helping Mom around the house and helping watch Sara and Emily."

Tyler was desperately afraid that if he laughed, he would have three sorely wounded children on his hands. Yet when he took a deep breath and considered things, he realized the question was rather mind-boggling.

"Let me get this straight." He looked from one to the other. "You kids are looking for ways to make money."

Three heads bobbed furiously.

While he understood their reasoning, their question was horizons beyond his experience with children. He hated to disappoint them, but for an instant he was at a total loss to give them an answer. "Well," he murmured, "why don't you tell me what kinds of things you do at home to help out? Maybe we can go from there."

Todd's mouth turned down. "I keep telling Mom I'm old enough to mow the lawn," he grumbled. "But she said I can't use a power lawn mower till next year."

Tyler seized upon the words as if they were heaven-sent. "Maybe not," he said mildly. "But a lot of people hate to rake their grass after it's mowed. I know I planned to mow my lawn first thing Saturday morning, but I'm not looking forward to raking it."

"I'll do it," the boy said eagerly.

Tyler winked at him. "Sounds good to me."

Todd's eyes were alight. "I'll bet there's lots of people in the neighborhood that don't like to pull weeds. Me and Sam could do that, too."

"And maybe wash cars," put in Sam. "Mom likes it when we wash our car, 'cause then she doesn't have to do it. Maybe we could set up a lemonade stand, too!"

Trisha, however, looked crushed. "I want to help, too," she said quaveringly. "But I don't know if I can do all that."

Tyler was touched. "I'll bet you'll be a big help," he said gently. "And I'm sure Todd and Samantha will split whatever they earn with you." For a second it appeared as if Todd would argue, so Tyler added firmly, "Of course, you might not earn quite as much, because you wouldn't be doing quite as much work."

"That sounds fair to me," Todd admitted.

Trisha seemed mollified. "Hey," she said excitedly. "I can sweep sidewalks. I've got my own broom and dustpan." She laid two small hands upon Tyler's knees. "How 'bout if I do yours?"

"They certainly need it," he assured her gravely.

Samantha jumped up. "I know what else I can do, too. What if I brushed Missy every day for you? I got a book at the library about shelties, and they need to be brushed a lot so their coat doesn't get matted."

"It would also take out a lot of the loose hair so she doesn't shed as much, either."

"And I could take her for walks, too, so she gets lots of exercise."

"That would certainly be helpful. I might not always have time to walk her." He just couldn't bear to burst Samantha's bubble.

"I could play with her, too...in my book it said shelties like to play with a Frisbee." She frowned suddenly. "Do you have a Frisbee?"

Her tone was so worried that Tyler almost lost it. *One Frisbee coming up,* he thought to himself. But before he could say a word, Trisha turned bright eyes up to him. "I've got one in my toy box. You can have it if I can play with Missy too, sometimes."

Tyler chuckled. "Well, kids, it looks like you've lined up your first customer."

He shook his head as he watched the trio race home again. He was a sucker for three pairs of eyes...as well as for the pretty lady who was their mother. It seemed the Lawrence clan was doing a pretty good job of shaking his world up just a little.

WEDNESDAY of that same week found Cass ready to pull her hair out. Emily was teething, and for the second day in a row she cried most of the morning. Cass breathed a sigh of relief when she finally got her down for her nap.

But it seemed Brian and Todd were determined to take up where Emily had left off. The two boys had been striking sparks off one another the entire morning. Cass stopped one argument and Katie another. She finally sent the three boys down to the park to play. Ever mindful of Tyler, she'd kept the kids amused inside these last few days. But the girls were also chomping at the bit, so she'd decided to take a chance. She'd sent Katie into the backyard with Sam and Sara, with strict instructions to keep their voices down.

But the three boys had no sooner returned than Cass heard the crash of a bicycle in the driveway, followed by several angry shouts. She peered out the window to see Todd racing after Brian, who ran into the backyard. By the time she ran out after them, Todd was charging Brian, head down like a raging bull.

Sara shrilled like a banshee when the two boys plowed through the sandbox, landing on the other side with a dull thud. As Cass grabbed their elbows and pulled them apart, she cast a desperate look at Tyler's place, praying he didn't have his windows open.

The two boys glared at each other, while Cass glared at the two of them. "All right," she said firmly. "Which one of you started this?"

"He did," Brian told her sullenly. "He called me a fathead!"

Cass's lips tightened. "Is that true, Todd?"

Head down, the boy nodded.

She took a deep breath. "All right, then," she said, keeping her voice very low. "Todd, you're confined to your room the rest of the afternoon—alone. Brian, I want you in the living room. And I want both of you to think about why you shouldn't call each other names, because the next time this happens, you two are going to kiss and make up."

Brian looked startled. Todd looked horrified. "We can't do that!" he cried. "That's—that's sissy!"

"Is it, now?" Her tone was crisp and to the point. "Then from now on maybe you two will try a little harder to get along, because that's exactly what you two will be doing, the next time something like this happens."

The two exchanged disbelieving glances as she marched them toward the house. Cass had a devil of a time holding back a smile of pure satisfaction.

That wasn't the case later in the evening, though. Cass was very much afraid the ruckus they'd made had disturbed Tyler. If it had, they owed him an apology. If not, she was going to have to make certain it never happened again. Either way, it would have made things infinitely easier for her if her newest neighbor had been a traveling salesman who spent very little time at home.

But the thought had no sooner popped into her mind than she experienced a faint stirring of guilt. She liked Tyler, she realized. He wasn't aloof or distant as she'd thought he might be. He was warm and likable and fun to be with. Oh, yes, she liked him indeed. Maybe a little too much for her own good....

Which only made the situation that much harder.

Since Todd had started the fight with Brian, Cass decided they might as well be in this together. He lagged behind her as she approached Tyler's front door. She fixed him with a glance he was very familiar with and he stepped up his pace. Together they mounted the wide front steps. She suspected they both felt as if they were approaching the hangman's noose.

But there was nothing tentative in the way she rang the doorbell and stood her ground in front of the door.

Inside the house, Missy began to bark. There was the sound of footsteps and the door opened.

"Cass." A warm, welcoming smile spread across Tyler's lips. "What a nice surprise."

It was all Cass could do not to catch her breath. Tyler looked as handsome, as coolly elegant as ever in slacks and shirt. The sun was skimming the treetops in the west, but it was still as blazingly hot as it had been all day. No one had a right to look that good when it was this hot. No one had a right to look that good, period.

She, on the other hand, felt like a wilted flower. She regretted that she hadn't taken the time to change into clean shorts and top; she was just as dismayed to realize she was far more conscious of her appearance than she would have liked.

"Hello, Tyler." She shoved a wayward strand of hair behind her ear. "If this isn't a bad time, Todd and I were wondering if we could talk to you for a minute."

Even before she finished speaking, the door opened wider. Cass found herself standing beside Todd in Tyler's entryway. The door had closed firmly behind her before she was even aware of it.

It was no wonder Tyler looked so cool. Apparently the house had central air-conditioning. She thought of her own tiny window air conditioner. It had gone out even before the dishwasher.

"Believe it or not, I was just thinking about you."

"Understandable, under the circumstances."

His smile was puzzled.

Cass decided to just go ahead and come out with it. She drew herself up proudly and glanced at Todd, who was staring at the toes of his tennis shoes as if they were utterly fascinating.

"We had a little problem at home this afternoon," she said evenly. "Todd and Brian—one of the boys I sit for—got into a rip-roaring fight that I'm sure you and half the neighborhood probably heard."

Tyler's smile faded. He appeared to hesitate. "Yes," he said slowly. "I'm afraid I did."

Cass squeezed Todd's shoulder. The boy stepped forward. "I didn't mean to bother you, honest. Mom's been telling us all week to keep it quiet when we're outside." He ventured a peek at Tyler, his expression sheepish. "I guess I just forgot. I'm sorry, Mr. Grant."

Mr. Grant. This was serious business, then. Tyler's lips twitched in spite of himself. He was secretly glad Cass had broached the subject, though. He'd been racking his brain most of the afternoon, trying to figure out how to approach her without hurting her feelings.

She took up again where Todd had left off, her lovely features grim. "To tell you the truth," she told him, her voice very low, "when you told me you worked here at home, I was afraid trying to keep eight kids quiet might be a problem."

Tyler felt a slight tug at his heart. For once her gaze wasn't quite so direct. Watching her arm slide around Todd's shoulders, he sensed how difficult this was for her.

"Aha," he said lightly. "Have you leaped onto the bandwagon with Suzanne? She keeps trying to tell me I don't belong here."

Cass frowned. "Suzanne?"

"The woman who was here last week." He lifted his eyes heavenward and shook his head. "I've been praying she'll stay in Chicago where she belongs and stop pestering me to come back."

Cass's heart beat faster. He was talking about Ms. Sexy Brunette. He didn't sound overly pleased with her—or was that only wishful thinking?

She lowered her lashes, trying not to show what she was feeling. "Oh," she murmured. "You mean your girlfriend."

Tyler laughed, the sound deep and rich. "She's not my girlfriend, Cass. She's just a friend, but she can be a nuisance. Especially when she keeps trying to run my life."

Cass couldn't help it. Her heart zipped skyward.

Tyler tipped his head to the side. "So," he said teasingly. "Are you in league with her? She'd like to see me jump ship and head back to Chicago."

"Of course not."

She smiled at him, a brilliant smile that held the light of a thousand suns. She didn't smile like that nearly enough, he decided. He wanted very much to see her smile like that again . . . and know that he was the reason behind it.

"Good," he said softly. "Because I happen to like living here."

"Noisy neighbors and all?" She didn't give him a chance to respond. He was disappointed when her smile withered and she sighed. "I'll bet you'll be glad when summer is over and the kids are back in school."

Tyler's smile faded, as well. "Cass," he said gently, "I don't expect miracles. And I'm sure we can meet halfway on this."

"But you have a living to make."

"And you have a job to do." He mulled for a few seconds. "My day usually ends at three o'clock, since that's when Wall Street closes. Morning is my busiest time."

Todd piped up. "We usually watch TV in the morning. And play games and stuff like that." He glanced at his mother. "Me and Dave and Brian start soccer practice over at the park next week at one o'clock."

"That lasts nearly an hour and a half," Cass reflected thoughtfully.

"I doubt this is an insurmountable problem, after all." Tyler lifted both brows. "Nor can I reasonably expect you to keep eight children cooped up inside your house the rest of the summer. We might as well handle this as painlessly as possible, which is why I think I'll move my office to the other side of the house. I could put my office where the den is and the den where my office is now."

"That will certainly help," she admitted. Her eyes remained troubled. "But it's not right that you have to go to so much trouble because of us."

He shrugged. "It's not that much trouble. I wouldn't even be giving up any space. And I can do it this weekend."

"No." She shook her head firmly. "I'll pitch in and help, and *we* will do it this weekend."

Tyler might have argued if he hadn't caught sight of the determined glint in her eyes. "First thing after lunch on Saturday sound okay?"

"I'll help, too." Todd started to step forward eagerly, then Tyler saw a hint of uncertainty flash across his face. "You aren't mad 'cause I made so much noise this afternoon, are you? What I mean is . . . you haven't changed your mind about me raking your lawn, have you? I could do that and then help move your office."

Tyler felt himself softening. He knew instinctively that Todd was not a troublemaker.

He laid a hand upon the boy's shoulder and shook his head. "I'll be upset if you *don't* rake my lawn for me."

Todd grinned broadly. "Thanks." He glanced at his mother. "I'll see you later, Mom. Mrs. Reed wants me to hoe her garden for her."

Cass blinked. Todd and the two youngest girls had told her yesterday that they intended to try to do some odd jobs around the neighborhood. She'd been certain the effort wouldn't last beyond the planning stage. But she hadn't realized they had already talked to Tyler, and somehow she wasn't quite sure how she felt about that.

Just as Todd dashed through the doorway, Tyler glimpsed two small figures outside. "Uh-oh," he murmured unthinkingly. "Here come the troops."

Sure enough, Trisha and Sam were barreling up the sidewalk. Footsteps pounded along the porch. Tyler was already at the door, holding it open.

Cass sighed, wondering a little at the broom Trisha carried. "Didn't I tell you two to stay at home?"

"We didn't come 'cause you're here." Sam dismissed her mother and beamed at Tyler, her chest swelling importantly. "I came to brush Missy and take her for a walk. And Trisha's gonna sweep Tyler's sidewalk."

Cass didn't know whether to laugh or cry. Nor was there time to get a word in edgewise, because Tyler had disappeared into the kitchen, the two girls and Missy trailing along behind him.

When he reappeared, Cass folded her arms across her chest and regarded him with a mock glare. "Why," she asked dryly, "do I have the feeling that instead of you recruiting them, the three of them managed to recruit you?"

He held up both hands in a conciliatory gesture. "Is that what you think?"

"I certainly do."

"Then think again, Mother dear, because when they came over last evening, we had a nice little chat."

"A nice little chat!" Now she was downright suspicious. "About what?"

His lips quirked. "What else? They had no trouble with investment objectives, but strategy was another matter."

"Investment objectives?" Cass narrowed her eyes. "Like bicycles, for instance? Skateboards and puppies?" She didn't give him a chance to answer. "And I suppose they expect a little monetary reward for their efforts?"

He looked surprised. "Is there something wrong with that?"

Her sigh reflected her frustration. "I don't want them to be a burden on anyone."

A burden. It was an odd choice of words, he decided. He frowned, vaguely disturbed. In the fraction of a second allotted him, his mind recorded a fleeting impression of hurt before her gaze slid away.

"Hey," he chided gently. "Don't be so touchy. I thought they were being rather resourceful."

"But I don't want them making a nuisance of themselves. Especially when I know you're not used to having so many kids around."

He reached out and caught her hand. "If that happens, you'll be the first to know." He saluted smartly. "Scout's honor."

She hadn't meant to smile; it just happened. "Tyler, that's a military salute. Weren't you ever a Boy Scout?"

"I'm afraid that's an honor I missed." His smile turned his eyes a toasty shade of gold. Cass felt her heart turn over.

"I suppose you were too busy making sure you got into Harvard Business School."

"Not on your life," he countered smoothly. "I happen to be a Yale man."

"Yale man or no, I'd feel better if you'd promise you'll let me know if things get out of hand with the kids."

"I promise," he said softly. His eyes gauged the shape and texture of her mouth. This was one promise he'd have liked to seal with a kiss.

"We're all done," announced a cheery little voice. "Can we take Missy for a walk now?"

"Sure thing, Samantha. Just let me get Missy's leash." It was an effort to speak normally. Tyler reluctantly dragged his gaze away from the tempting swell of parted lips gone soft. Would Cass have welcomed his kiss? Oh, Lord. Just thinking about it made his gut twist with desire, a desire so strong and unexpected it caught him wholly off guard.

In the end, Tyler decided he'd better go along with the girls this first time to make certain Missy didn't get away from them. He asked Cass to come along as well, but she politely declined.

Watching her progress down the sidewalk back to her house, Tyler admitted to a nagging disappointment. He also found himself pondering his involuntary response to her, but his mind balked at the obvious answer.

Surely he wasn't falling for her. It was improbable. Impossible. Downright crazy. She had four small children, for heaven's sake!

So why, he asked himself grimly, did he have the feeling that where Cass Lawrence was concerned, he was going to have a hell of a time keeping his hands on the table?

6

THREE DAYS LATER, Cass had decided that helping Tyler move his office hadn't been such a good idea, after all. It wasn't the fact that three of her four children had traipsed along with her, delightedly informing her that Sam and Trisha were going to wash Tyler's car while Todd did some jobs around the yard. Nor did the idea of a little hard work put her off. In fact, she would have been grateful in the extreme, if he hadn't insisted on moving almost everything himself.

This was the first time she'd seen him in jeans. She'd been so surprised when he opened his door that she had simply stared. Her gaze took in his lightweight cotton shirt and trickled slowly down muscular legs that seemed impossibly long and lean, tucked snugly into worn denim. When her eyes finally made the return trip to his face, she discovered a knowing half smile on his lips. A rare but incriminating blush flooded her cheeks; she hadn't realized her inventory of him had been so tellingly thorough.

Now, half an hour later, she leaned against the door frame and watched him wrestle an armchair across the floor to the place where his bookcase had been. Once again it struck her just how good-looking he was. Seeing the muscles in his legs tighten and flex made her think of all things blatant and sexual and very, very male . . . and touched off a corresponding tingle in all that was female within her. It was an awareness that Cass hadn't experienced in a long, long time.

When she blew out a long sigh, Tyler glanced at her. She folded her arms across her chest and fixed him with a glare. "I thought you were going to let me help."

He straightened with a lift of his brows. "You are," he informed her mildly.

She pulled a face. "How?"

"You can help me decide how to arrange the furniture. And as long as we're on the subject, you make for an extremely fetching decorative touch."

When his eyes slid appreciatively over her form, clad in simple cotton shorts and a cap-sleeved T-shirt, she felt the heat of his gaze all through her. Her tongue felt glued to the roof of her mouth, and she sought vainly for something cute, something glib to say in return. But it had been ages since she'd played these light flirtatious games, so long she wasn't sure she knew the rules anymore.

It wasn't until Tyler turned his attention to his massive desk that she found her voice. He'd managed to move the desk only five or six inches in as many minutes. "Are you ready to throw in the towel yet?"

He turned to regard her, hands braced at his hips, legs spread carelessly apart in a ruggedly male stance. "You," he proclaimed, eyes alight with laughter, "are what's known as an ego-deflater. I wasn't opposed to having my new neighbor think I was all brawn and no brains. But I'll admit right about now I could use another hand."

"I'll not only give you a helping hand, I'll throw in a little advice, too. Let's take the drawers out and put a couple of rugs under the legs, so we can slide it along."

"That's the easy way out," he said accusingly.

"No," she said and laughed. "That's the smart way out."

A short time later Tyler gave the sofa a final nudge. He dropped onto the cushions and leaned his head back wearily, stretching his legs before him. With the back of one hand he wiped the perspiration from his brow and cast a pained glance at Cass. "I've discovered a new respect for the movers who delivered my furniture. Lord, my back aches!"

Cass had collapsed into a chair five minutes ago, but she couldn't resist teasing him. "What happened to the guy who was determined to impress me with all his brawn?"

His eyes took on a decided gleam. "I'll just have to find another way," he retorted.

Cass chuckled. She had to give him credit—he didn't miss a beat. She glanced out the window at the driveway, where Samantha and Trisha were rinsing the soap from Tyler's car. Todd was busy raking grass, but Trisha saw her and gave her a soapy wave, her hand clutching a sopping rag.

Katie was at her friend Brenda's this afternoon, but Cass's three youngest had been in and out of Tyler's place half a dozen times. It warmed her heart to notice that Tyler didn't appear nearly as bowled over by her children as he had been at first.

Feeling a little impish, she let a worried frown appear as she continued to gaze at the two girls. "Oh, dear," she murmured, putting just the right note of concern into her voice. "I hope you remembered to roll up the windows before letting the girls wash your car."

Her timing couldn't have been better. His gaze veered toward the window. Cass saw his eyes widen when he saw the spray of water gushing at the side of his car. His look of panic was precious. He was up and out the door in nothing flat. When he reappeared in the doorway seconds later, Cass was still convulsed with laughter.

"Not only are you an ego-deflater," he declared, "but you have a mean streak in you, Cass Lawrence. I was arbitrarily informed by your daughter Samantha that 'Mommy told us to *always* make sure the windows are up before we wash the car.'"

The sound of her laughter rippled through the air. "For a guy who was complaining his back ached, you managed to move like a streak of lightning."

"Thanks to you," he retorted.

He advanced slowly toward her. Cass reacted unthinkingly, jumping up and fleeing to the opposite wall, but he pursued her relentlessly. His movements slow and deliberate, mock-threatening, he planted one palm flat against the wall behind her, and then the other so that she was trapped between his arms.

"Tyler!" she gasped. "What do you think you're doing?"

His grin was positively devilish. "I believe it's called getting even."

One minute she was laughing, playfully protesting and demanding that he move. But suddenly, in the instant between one breath and the next, everything changed.

Her laughter died in her throat. Tyler's smile faded slowly. Her eyes strayed helplessly to his face, its strong, angular features etched in the brilliant glow of the sun. The chestnut richness of his hair lay tumbled across his forehead. She couldn't look away from his mouth, so masculine, but beautifully chiseled.

Cass pressed her hands flat against the wall behind her. It was all she could do not to slide her arms around his neck. Her breathing wavered. "Tyler..."

"Don't," he whispered. "Don't say anything."

She found it nearly impossible to breathe and held herself perfectly still, yet could feel his closeness with all that she possessed. His nearness surrounded, took hold of her. They touched nowhere; they touched everywhere. She saw in his face the same shattering awareness that had seized her. At that knowledge, a quickening heat stormed through her.

Her heart stood still as his head descended with an excruciating slowness. By the time his mouth met hers, her nerves were tightened to an almost painful pitch of awareness. At first he simply brushed his lips across her own, as if testing and gauging her reaction. She let her lashes flutter closed.

Swamped by sensation, every cell in her body aquiver, Cass felt shaky and tremulous inside. She had wondered what it would be like if Tyler kissed her; now she knew, and reality topped expectation a hundredfold.

His kiss was infinitely gentle, infinitely knowing, sweet but subtly masterful, confirming what she already suspected—Tyler was a man who knew his way around women. She dug her nails into her palms as she fought the urge to wrap her arms around his neck once again.

"Nice," he murmured in a voice that made her tremble all over again. His mouth hovered a mere breath above hers. "Very nice, Cass Lawrence." His mouth slid to the corners of her lips, first one and then the other.

His hands slid down to her waist, drawing her near and angling her body flush against his. This time when he reclaimed her lips, the pressure was deeper, firmer and sweetly urgent.

Cass was lost. Her hands lifted of their own accord. Her fingers curled into his shoulders, loving the knotted tension of muscle and bone. It had been so long since she had been held like this...too long. With a tiny little moan she sighed and gave herself up to the wondrously secure feeling of being held close and tight against a warm, male body.

Time and place ceased to exist. She was so caught up in the swirling mists of pleasure that she scarcely heard the insistent jangling in the background. It wasn't until Tyler released her mouth and lifted his head that she realized the intrusive sound was the ringing of the telephone.

He smiled at her; Cass still felt dazed. His hands slid up to cup her shoulders; he guided her several steps and gently pushed her down and onto the sofa, then bent and kissed the tip of her nose. "Keep my seat warm," he whispered.

He picked up the phone in the kitchen, just around the corner. Trying to gather her scattered wits, Cass rose and ambled about the room. The last thing she intended was to eavesdrop on Tyler's conversation, but she caught a glimpse of him standing with his back toward her. She saw him shift the receiver from one ear to the other.

"Suzanne," he began.

Reality staked its claim with a vengeance. Cass stood stock-still, feeling as if the wind had been knocked from her. There was a painful catch in her heartbeat as she turned away, her steps directed toward the front door. She eased it shut with a quiet click and stepped into the sunlight so bright it was almost obscene.

In the kitchen, Tyler grimaced. A scowl creased his brow as his eyes sought the clock on the wall. "Suzanne," he said briskly, his patience strained to the limit. "If this is the only reason you called, you might as well save your breath.... No, I'm not being rude, I'm being honest...." He listened a few seconds, then uttered a tight laugh. "I can see why you've never traded in futures, Suzanne. Just remember I told you it'll never happen."

With that Tyler dropped the receiver back into the cradle. His smile was once again in place as he strode back into the den.

Cass was gone.

Tyler rushed to the window in time to see her say something to Todd, then point toward home. A minute later she was back in her own house.

The curtain fell back into place. Tyler didn't need to ask why Cass had left so abruptly; the rigidly proud set of her shoulders told him all he needed to know....

He cursed long and loudly. Suzanne couldn't have picked a worse time to call.

HOW COULD a day that started out so well end up so miserably?

Cass tried telling herself she didn't care who Tyler Grant chose to conduct his affairs with, as long as it wasn't her. For the life of her, she couldn't think why he'd bothered to kiss her. No doubt he missed Ms. Sexy Brunette—Suzanne—and had decided to settle for whatever was available.

But she, Cass Lawrence, was definitely not available. Besides, she told herself stoutly, she didn't want or need a man sniffing around her heels. It was the male of the species that had caused her so much trouble in the first place!

Katie got back from Brenda's just a few minutes later. Today was considerably cooler than the past few days had been, so she slipped a meat loaf into the oven. She smiled wickedly as she jammed the oven door shut. Rick had always hated her meat loaf. Unimaginative, he'd called it. What, she wondered snidely, would Tyler Grant think?

Cass had given Todd, Trisha and Samantha strict instructions to come home as soon as they finished Tyler's car. She'd been keeping one ear tuned for their arrival, but they were taking so long, she was afraid she was going to have to send Katie after them.

At precisely that moment the front door banged. Trisha's chatter immediately filtered into the kitchen, but Cass was caught wholly off guard by the sound of a deep male voice. Startled, her eyes met Katie's, just as Todd whizzed through the swinging door that separated the kitchen from the living room.

"Mom! You don't care if Tyler stays for dinner, do you?"

Cass blinked. Then she narrowed her eyes. "Don't tell me you already asked him," she said tightly.

Todd bit his lip. "Well . . . sort of."

A honey-colored brow shot up. "Sort of?"

"Yeah, I did . . . or rather, *we* did. Me and Sam and Trish."

Cass longed to moan aloud. Instead she sighed, yanked off her oven mitt and dropped it onto the counter.

Samantha tugged at her sleeve. "We didn't think you'd mind, 'cause you're always telling us it's all right if we invite a friend to stay for dinner once in a while."

"Tyler doesn't like to eat alone," Todd put in earnestly.

"And he burns everything he cooks." Trisha giggled.

"And he likes you, Mom." Sam turned huge brown eyes up to her. "He likes you a lot."

"Good grief," she muttered. "I could almost believe he coached the three of you!" Yet how could she refuse such innocent faces?

"That he does," echoed a now-familiar voice from behind her. "He also thinks she's very pretty."

Cass wasn't in the mood for sugary sweet talk. Still, it took every ounce of willpower she possessed to turn and face him. "There's no need to go that far," she stated smoothly. "Of course you're welcome to stay for dinner."

Sam and Trish clapped their hands. Todd let out a whoop, while Katie simply smiled. Tyler's gaze rested warmly on Cass. "Something smells great. What are we having?"

A spurt of vindictive satisfaction shot through her. "Meat loaf," she informed him almost challengingly.

If she had been hoping for a reaction, the one she got certainly wasn't the one she expected. He rubbed his hands together and glanced at the kids. "One of my favorites," he proclaimed heartily.

Todd was already tugging at his sleeve. "Can I show you my matchbox-car collection?"

Cass watched as her three children guided him through the swinging door once more, then rolled her eyes. She suspected Tyler might change his mind by the time the night was over. "Maybe this is just what he needs," she muttered darkly. "Let him get a behind-the-scenes look at the Lawrence clan, and we'll see just how eager he is for a repeat performance."

When she turned around, Katie stood behind her, one hand cupped over her mouth. Cass scowled. "Don't you dare laugh, young lady."

Katie shook her head. "I wasn't going to laugh, Mom. I was going to say I told you so. I knew he liked you right from the start."

Cass thumped a pan onto the stove. "Katie," she warned, "one of these days you're going to learn that some men will say anything to get what they want."

When Katie went to set the table, she discovered G.I. Joe napkins were all that they had. She wailed long and loudly when her mother instructed her to use them, anyway; Cass smiled with perverse satisfaction when Tyler sat down at the table and did a double take when he reached for his napkin.

But to her everlasting annoyance, she couldn't find a single fault with either the kids' behavior or their manners throughout the meal. As soon as they had finished, the kids carried their plates to the sink and rinsed them under the tap. But when Katie started to clear the rest of the table, Tyler stood and slanted her a smile. "Why don't you run along?" he suggested. "I'd be glad to help your mom with these."

Cass opened her mouth just as Tyler's gaze swiveled to her. "I know," he said and chuckled. "I'm spoiling her, right?" A slow grin crept across his lips, crooked and utterly disarming.

Her jaw closed with a snap. Cass swore silently. Damn! Why did he have to be so likable? So irresistible? It wasn't fair, she raged. It wasn't fair at all.

She raked back her chair and moved to the sink, where she dropped a handful of silverware with a clatter.

Tyler sighed and set a soiled casserole dish upon the counter. "Would you like to tell me what's got you on the warpath?"

"Not a thing." She shoved the handle on the faucet. The ensuing spray of water into the sink was so forceful it spattered the front of her blouse. She uttered a few choice words under her breath.

He propped a hip against the counter next to her and folded his arms over his chest. "I don't suppose it has anything to do with a bothersome phone call that I happened to get this afternoon."

Bothersome! I'll bet, Cass thought scathingly. The man knew just what to say, all right—only she wasn't buying it. "You're imagining things," she stated flatly.

"If I am, then maybe you'd like to explain why you left without even saying goodbye."

"You were busy."

"And you, dear lady, are jealous."

Jealous! Cass whipped her head around and glared at him. She wasn't angry. She wasn't jealous. No, if anything she was furious for offering herself so—so willingly! She plunged the casserole dish into the sudsy dishwater. Water sloshed over the edge of the sink. By now the bottom third of her shirt was soaked.

"How—" she posed the question stiffly "—could I possibly be jealous, when there's nothing between us?"

"Nothing between us." He shook his head, his tone gently chiding. "Aren't you forgetting the matter of one particular kiss shared only this afternoon?"

"What kiss?" she inquired airily.

His smile was maddening. "I'd be more than happy to refresh your memory." His hand was on her nape, shocking in its warmth, startling in the way his touch filled her with an insidious, melting heat.

She jerked away, spattering them both with dishwater. Cass grabbed the nearest towel and wiped her hands. All the while she glared at him fiercely.

Tyler sighed and dropped his hand to his side. "You know," he said softly, "I was very disappointed when I got off the phone and found you gone." When she said nothing, a sheepish look flitted across his features. "And yes, I did coach the kids just a little to get them to ask me to stay for dinner."

"So you're manipulative, too!"

"Not manipulative, just desperate." Under any other circumstances, his smile would have made her heart turn over. "Is that so hard to believe?"

The answer was a resounding yes. "I'm sure this is all very amusing to you, Tyler Grant." Her voice came out low and taut, she knew. "Is it too much to ask for a little honesty? I'd much rather be hurt than lied to, so let's just drop all the fun and games, all right? I left because I didn't think you'd want me around while you talked to Suzanne." To her horror, her vision began to mist.

She nearly cringed when Tyler closed the gap between them. He slipped his knuckles beneath her chin and slowly guided her eyes to his. To her surprise, all the laughter was gone from his face. His probing gaze reflected an intensity that shook her to the core.

He shook his head slightly. "I told you the other night Suzanne was just a friend. Didn't you believe me?"

What did he expect her to say? Suzanne was a tough act to follow. Oh, damn, maybe she *was* jealous of her. Maybe Suzanne was only one of many beautiful women that he knew. She couldn't compete with any of them, so why pretend otherwise?

Confronting the truth really wasn't as painful as she'd feared. But admitting it to Tyler was something else entirely.

"Look," she said finally. "You don't have to explain your relationships to me, past, present or otherwise."

Tyler regarded her silently, watching her gaze slide painfully away from him. Her head was down, her hair was up again leaving the nape of her neck bare. There was something very vulnerable about her pose just then, something that set him back on his heels. Cass had struck him so far as a very strong, capable woman. Yet he felt a surge of protectiveness swell deep inside him, an instinct he hadn't even known he possessed.

Once again he touched his fingers to her chin, responding to the uncertainty he sensed beneath her facade of control.

When he spoke, his tone was very quiet. "I'll be honest with you, Cass, because I think maybe I should clear this up, once and for all. I *was* involved with Suzanne a long time ago—years ago. But that's all over now, though we've remained friends. We both know we could never go back, and furthermore, neither one of us wants to."

He paused. "There's nothing between me and Suzanne," he repeated. "Nor will there be." The pad of his thumb skimmed her cheekbone. "Do you believe me?"

He raised her chin again, so she was forced to look at him directly. She nodded, her eyes clinging to his, wide and very blue. He wondered if she had any idea just what her expression did to his insides. A part of him longed to wrap her close and ease the elusive hurt he sensed in her. Another part of him wanted to crush her against him, part those raspberry-colored lips and grant his mouth and hands free rein.

Instead he guided a gilded curl behind her ear. It wrapped around his finger with a will of its own, and he had to fight the urge to linger. "Maybe," he said lightly, "we'd better get these dishes done before Katie comes in here and finds me slacking off on the job." A lean finger lifted to trace the tip-tilted outline of her nose and rest for a heart-stopping moment in the center of her mouth. "One of you might be tempted to find a replacement for me, and I can't have that now, can I?"

His hand deserted her. Cass battled an unreasoning disappointment that he hadn't kissed her again; it was keener still when he walked to the front door as soon as they'd tidied up the kitchen.

She and the kids followed. She hated to see him leave, but she wouldn't ask him to stay. Pride kept the words buried deep inside.

He pivoted just outside the door. Even though he was one step below her, Cass had to angle her gaze slightly upward to meet his. She found his eyes examining her, not critically, but with a heated intimacy that made her feel all tremulous and weak inside. She found herself reliving that poignantly sweet moment this afternoon, when he'd kissed her.

He spoke for her ears alone. "Why don't you come home with me for a while?"

There was no mistaking the message in his eyes. If she went with him, she had no doubt that they would take up exactly where they'd left off this afternoon. And she wanted to go with him. Lord, how she wanted to! But the intensity of that very need frightened her.

"We rented a movie, and I told the kids I'd watch it with them."

Cass met his gaze with difficulty. Did she only imagine the faint chastisement in his expression? She experienced a prickly defensiveness. Darn it, he didn't have to make her feel so—so guilty about it! Sure, she enjoyed his company. And yes, she was divorced and sleeping alone these days. But that didn't give him the right to think she would hop into the sack with the first available man that came along.

She was immediately ashamed of herself. Tyler had been a perfect gentleman so far. He'd given her no reason to believe he was dying to get her into bed.... Something caught inside her chest. She balked at the obvious.... Surely she wasn't disappointed? Or was she?

"Good night, Tyler." From somewhere she summoned a smile. He didn't try to convince her further, and for that she was glad. The girls waved when he paused to look back over his shoulder a few seconds later.

There was a mirror in the small entryway, and Cass caught sight of herself the instant she closed the door. She paused to consider her reflection.

She wished she hadn't.

Dressed as she was in shorts and T-shirt, her hair caught up in a ponytail, she was definitely not the type to be seen with a sophisticate like Tyler Grant.

Yet she couldn't deny the magnetic pull she felt when she was around him. It wasn't just that he was thoughtful and sweet and got along surprisingly well with her kids. He was surprisingly down-to-earth and practical. The day of Todd and Brian's uproar, he could have made her life miserable, indeed, if he'd chosen to be difficult. Instead he'd tried to make things easier for her.

Cass couldn't help it. For a moment she let herself be swept away with him on a cloud of moondust, just the two of them, Cass Lawrence and Tyler Grant. It was a wonderful image. Wonderful, but hardly realistic.

7

IF TYLER WAS OUT to torment her, he was doing a bang-up job.

Scarcely a day went by over the next few weeks that she didn't see him. He appeared at her cooking classes; he tagged along on their Sunday picnic at the park, after Todd begged to ask him to come along. He showed up nearly every evening so Samantha could walk Missy—usually just when Cass and Katie were tackling the dishes. Most of the time Tyler ended up drying dishes instead of Katie, leading Cass to needle him that he was indeed trying to spoil her daughter.

She liked him more with every day that passed. He made her laugh, no matter how tired or down she was feeling. She was coming to depend upon him not only as a friend, but as a part of her life that would be sorely missed if he were to leave.... And that frightened her like nothing else could have.

Because try as she might, she couldn't quite banish her disturbing awareness of him. She couldn't be with him without wanting him to touch her again, to kiss her again the way he had that long-ago day. Sometimes she thought he was just as confused as she was. More than once she caught him staring at her when he thought she wasn't looking. And she stared just as hungrily when she was sure *he* wasn't looking.

Why was he bothering with her? With all of them? How long would it be before he decided to turn his attention elsewhere? All those questions—and more—gnawed at her.

The second Saturday in July was no different from any other. She always spent weekends catching up on all the little jobs that couldn't be done while she was baby-sitting during the week.

Trisha and Samantha were sitting on a blanket spread beneath a tree when Tyler wandered over.

"Hello, ladies."

Trisha giggled and poked her sister. "Did you hear that, Sam? He called us ladies."

He peered down at the mound of tiny, frilly clothes piled between them. "I think that's a pretty apt title, considering you're involved in such feminine endeavors."

They looked at him as if he'd lost his mind.

He grinned and gestured at the clothes. "Playing dolls," he clarified. "It's something all girls do, right?"

"We're not playing any old *dolls*," he was indignantly informed. "We're playing with our Barbie dolls."

"Oh." He smothered a laugh. Was there a difference? Apparently. "Where's your mom today?" he asked.

"She's in the garage," he was told. Leaving them to their activities, he walked off. He stopped short, however, at the sight that met his eyes in the garage. Long, slender legs and pink-tipped toenails peeped out from beneath the front end of Cass's station wagon.

"Cass!"

Under the car, Cass froze when she heard an unfamiliar bellow. Hard, precise footsteps drummed along the concrete floor. Moving her head a scant inch, she glimpsed immaculate leather loafers closing in on her.

A second later an upside-down Tyler appeared beside the left front tire. "What," he asked, "do you think you're doing?"

Her smile was as weak as her voice, she knew. "Changing the oil."

She saw Tyler close his eyes and count to ten. "Would you please come out from under there so I can talk to you?"

He delivered his request with painstaking politeness. Cass wiggled out, suddenly irritated because she felt guilty as sin and couldn't think why on earth she felt that way!

When she had scooted clear of the bumper, a strong male hand reached out and hauled her to her feet. A twinge of embarrassment cut through her when Tyler proceeded to inspect the scraggly cutoffs and stained denim shirt she always wore when she changed the oil and filter in her car.

"Don't look at me like that," she said crossly. "I didn't just crawl out from under a rock."

His brows were arched in a way she could only call arrogant. Cass held her ground and gave him back look for look. For the life of her, she couldn't figure out why he appeared so annoyed.

"You," he said finally, "are unbelievable."

"Why is that?" If her tone was just a little defensive, she couldn't help it. She felt totally ridiculous, standing before him dressed as she was, her hands as grimy as the wrench she held.

"Why?" It didn't help when he looked at her as if she'd gone off the deep end. "For crying out loud, Cass, why don't you just take the damn car down to a service station?"

"Because I can do it for half the cost." She looked him straight in the eye.

Tyler grimaced. "Nonetheless, it's a man's job." He looked her straight in the eye.

She sent him a saccharine smile. "In case you hadn't noticed, there isn't a man around. Unless you want to count my ten-year-old son, of course."

"Correction," he parried, his tone as smooth as silk. "There *wasn't* a man around. But there is now, so why don't you just turn that wrench over to me?" He plucked the wrench from her grasp.

Her jaw sagged. Dear Lord, he had on a *white* shirt. "Tyler!" she exclaimed. "You—you can't change the oil in those clothes! They'll get all dirty!"

"Just watch me," was all he said.

Cass gaped when he proceeded to crawl beneath her car. Amid the clunking and thumping, there was a number of grittily voiced, colorful phrases. An hour later he dropped the hood into place and flashed a triumphant smile as he turned. He looked so pleased with himself, Cass couldn't bear to tell him she'd have finished in half the time.

She glanced up at him with a faint smile. "Do this often, do you?"

"Not for years, but now that I have, I won't bother taking my car in to the garage anymore."

Cass smothered a laugh. Tyler might be a wizard in the financial world, but she suspected he'd have a long way to go to make his mark as an auto mechanic. But she wanted to wail when she spied his shirt.

"Oh, Tyler. Just look at you! You've ruined a perfectly good shirt."

He glanced down at the dingy spots on his shirtfront. "It'll wash," he said and shrugged.

"That's what you think. Getting those spots out is hopeless. And as for you... you're impossible!" The lack of heat in her voice took the sting from the words.

A gleam lighted his eyes. "On the contrary," he murmured, "I'm beginning to think anything's possible. In fact, I think this is an excellent time to look at your dishwasher."

"My dishwasher!"

"There seems to be an echo in here." He glanced around the garage as if puzzled.

Cass planted her hands on her hips. The situation was no longer quite as amusing. "Tyler," she argued, "this is ridiculous. There's no reason for you to put yourself out for me this way."

"You may not feel the need," he countered with a devastating smile, "but I do. Besides, maybe it's just a minor problem."

The effect of that smile was totally wasted. "It's not," she predicted darkly, "so you might as well not even bother."

Tyler had already interpreted the warning signs on her features and released a gusty sigh—not a sound of defeat, but one of frustration. "Why are you being so stubborn?"

"Because it's not your problem!"

Tyler nearly groaned. He wondered if she had any idea how she affected him. They were so close he could see each enchanting freckle sprinkled across her nose;

his fingers longed to reach out and chart each curve of those sleek, sinewy legs of hers.

"Haven't you ever heard of the good-neighbor policy?"

"But this is above and beyond the call of duty!"

"I heartily disagree." He shook his head and stepped up to her, tapping the tip of her nose with his finger. "Don't frown so, Cass. I seem to recall hearing it causes wrinkles."

"Really." Her glare was blistering, but it didn't deter him in the least. Cass had no choice but to follow when he opened the door and stepped into the house.

Tyler pulled out the racks and dismantled the spray arm to see if there was anything trapped inside. He then removed the bottom panel and fiddled with the hoses, then stared in dismay at the maze of electrical wires. Twenty minutes later, his good humor had clearly disintegrated along with his good intentions.

He shoved himself back onto the balls of his feet. "Cripes!" he muttered. "This is hopeless!"

Somehow Cass refrained from saying *I told you so*. From her post at the kitchen table, she voiced a mild agreement. "That it is."

Tyler didn't say a word. He simply pushed himself up from the floor in one smooth, fluid motion. Cass watched, momentarily fascinated by his graceful economy of movement as he strode across her kitchen. It wasn't until he grabbed the phone book on the stand just inside the dining room that she realized his intention.

She scrambled to her feet. "What are you doing?"

"Calling a repairman." His tone matched the resolve on his face. He flipped the phone book open.

"But this is Saturday. It'll cost a fortune on a week-end!"

He was busy scanning the pages. "Cass," he murmured absently, "fixing that dishwasher is way over my head. And not all outfits are closed on Saturday. See, there's one right here." He reached for the phone.

Cass fairly flew across the floor. "No!"

"No?" Tyler was just a little annoyed by her stubbornness. "Why the hell not?" Brown eyes clashed fiercely with blue, and he didn't bother to conceal his irritation. "With so many kids on your hands, a dishwasher isn't a luxury, it's a necessity!"

Hot anger ricocheted through her. "Tell me about it!" she snapped. "Do you think I like having a chronic case of dishpan hands?" She splayed her fingers wide and grimaced. "I'd have called a repairman months ago, Tyler Grant, but in my case I'm afraid it *is* a luxury I just can't afford."

Stunned by her vehemence, Tyler stared at her. Then, as if she had just realized what she had said, a fleeting distress flashed across her features. She whirled abruptly, but he was quicker. He caught her arm and pulled her around once more.

"Cass." He spoke her name awkwardly, cursing himself for the heel he knew he was. He'd gladly have given her the money to repair the dishwasher, but knew she would never accept it. "I didn't mean to upset you, I swear."

To her everlasting shame, an unaccustomed ache had closed her throat. She sensed the probing of his eyes, but couldn't look at him, she just couldn't. "I know."

His gaze roved over her face. Her lashes shielded her expression from him, but her lips were trembling. If nothing else, he knew that Cass Lawrence was one tough lady. The sight of that tiny little quiver made his heart wrench.

"Cass." Tyler hesitated. He had the feeling she might not like what he was about to ask. "I don't mean to pry, but doesn't your ex-husband pay child support?"

Cass stiffened. She would have pulled away, but his hands captured her shoulders and held her firm. Every muscle in her body went rigid, but Tyler wasn't to be dissuaded so easily. His hands tightened their hold. Her resistance was slight as he pulled her toward him, but it was still there. When they stood face-to-face he wasn't surprised to discover her eyes flashing like a lighted fuse. Yet the oddest thought ran through his mind. Cass was quick to show her anger . . . but not her pain.

"I do my best," she informed him tautly. "And I dare you or anyone else to say I'm not a good mother."

Her defensiveness wasn't lost on Tyler. He was reminded of a mother hen rallying her chicks, and the thought made him smile. "You're not just a good mother, Cass. You're a wonderful mother." His smile faded. "I'm not criticizing. But if you're having trouble making ends meet, maybe you should see an attorney. Maybe your ex-husband's child-support payments should be increased."

Child support. Now that was rich. How could she possibly tell Tyler that when Rick had left, he'd headed for parts unknown . . . ? An almost hysterical laugh bubbled up inside her. Memories crowded in, the elusive hurt that was like a thorn inside her still. She wished she could be angry; it would have helped to wash away the bitter truth.

She sighed, and it was as if all the fight went out of her. Tyler took unfair advantage and wrapped his arms around her, easing her head down to his chest. "There isn't any child support," she stated quietly.

It took Tyler an instant to recover from the shock of that statement. "But you've got four kids.... Why the hell not?" Mingled with his incredulity was a virulent note of indignant outrage.

Cass gave a tiny shake of her head. "There just isn't." Her voice was so low he had to strain to hear.

And that, Tyler thought grimly, was that, even as a dozen unanswered questions tumbled through his mind. Unfortunately, he could see that Cass was not a woman to bare her soul so readily. He felt the tension invade her body once again and knew he'd pressed enough. If he probed any further, he was very much afraid she'd run for the hills.

His arms tightened instinctively. His fingers traced a soothing pattern down the length of her back and up again. A jolt of pleasure shot through him when her hands sneaked slowly around his waist. He liked the feel of her in his arms, all warm and trusting and kittenish, liked it far too much to shatter the peacefulness of the moment.

The moment was just as precious to Cass, also rather frightening. She'd felt so scared and alone when Rick left her; she had put up a good front for the sake of the kids, but it had taken her a long time to regain her courage and self-esteem. She was proud of her newfound independence and self-sufficiency. Sure, there were a few monetary stumbling blocks—like the hotwater heater and the dishwasher—but she hadn't lost faith in herself, by any means.

Yet she couldn't deny that being with Tyler like this felt so—so damned good! Even as she reminded herself staunchly that she didn't need a shoulder to lean on, she took comfort and strength from the sheltering protection of his arms around her, hard and tight. Surely it wouldn't hurt. Just this once . . .

Even the sound of the back door slamming didn't permeate her placid contentment. Footsteps pounded across the kitchen floor, only to stop abruptly. A second later the back door slammed again.

"Who was that?" Her voice was muffled. Her mouth was pressed against the warm hollow of his throat.

"Katie." He chuckled when she moaned into his chest. "For some unknown reason, I have the feeling I've just been given the seal of approval. Her eyes got round as saucers, but when she backed out, she was wearing a grin the size of Lake Michigan."

Tyler was pleased to notice Cass didn't budge even a hair. "Wonderful," she muttered. "Now I'm really in for it."

He kissed the baby-soft skin of her temple. "Why is that?"

Cass raised her head. "She seems to have this crazy idea that you . . ." She felt herself redden. " . . . and I . . . that you have this . . . oh, you know what I mean!"

"I do, and it's not so crazy, after all." He lowered his voice to a conspiratorial whisper. "Do you think Todd suspects I have this uncontrollable yearning for his mother? He might be tempted to come after me with his baseball bat."

"You're impossible." Cass thumped her fists against his chest, unable to hold back a laugh any longer. He promptly seized her wrists and pulled them around his neck.

"That's already been established," he parried smoothly. He lowered his head, making his intention obvious.

"Tyler!" She felt duty bound to object. "One of the kids could walk in any minute—"

Her protest was caught somewhere between her mouth and his. "One already has," he murmured, just before his mouth closed over hers.

His kiss was slow and languid, his lips both tempting and tasting as they sipped from hers. Cass felt as if she no longer had a will of her own. She sagged against him, her legs turning to jelly as his lips continued their sweet seduction.

Her mouth was moist and trembling when he finally drew back from her. Eyes shining, her cheeks flushed with pleasure, she obviously said the first thing that popped into her head. "You have oil on your cheek."

Tyler was relieved to note that the shadows had left her face. He intended to do everything in his power to see that they didn't return. He let her lean back in the circle of his arms, but didn't break his hold.

"So do you." He cocked an eyebrow and went on brashly. "Since we both need a shower, I have the perfect solution. My shower is big enough for two, and it will even save wear and tear on your new hot-water heater."

Her heart leaped. He was joking, of course. Dear Lord, if he wasn't . . . That was something that didn't bear thinking about! "Your shower is decadent," she informed him primly.

His lips twitched. "Decadent?"

"The glass in your shower door is completely clear! Why, you can see right through it! And your tub is easily big enough for two. Why, your whole bathroom is decadent!"

"And I suppose you think I'm debauched."

She frowned at him playfully. "I'm beginning to wonder!"

Certainly debauched was how he felt right now. His mind was having a field day at the thought of Cass in his shower—or in his tub, with him sitting right beside her.... It didn't take him long to decide a change of subject was in order.

He crossed to the doorway and cleared his throat. "Katie," he called, "could you come here for a minute?"

The girl appeared in the hallway.

He gave her his most charming smile. "How would you like to earn a little extra money baby-sitting your brother and sisters tonight? I think your mother could use a night off, so I thought I'd take her out for a while."

"Sounds okay by me." Katie grinned.

Cass still couldn't believe she'd heard right. She placed her hands on her hips and glared at him. "Tyler," she demanded, "just what do you think you're doing?"

The merest hint of a smile curved his lips. "Isn't it obvious? You need a breather—some time out just for yourself."

"And you've decided to see that I get it?" she asked after a moment.

"Exactly. For starters, we can go out for dinner and then take it from there."

Her gaze never wavered from his face. "Just you and me?" she asked slowly.

"Yes, indeed," he stated firmly. "Just you and me."

She didn't answer. Her expression was half accusing, half wary and wholly uncertain.

Tyler sighed. Why he was being so insistent, he didn't know. But he wanted to smooth those tiny worry lines between her brows and see her smile again. "I suppose you think I'm trying to get you alone," he remarked.

Her eyes narrowed. "Are you?"

His smile faded. "What if I am?" he asked very quietly.

Her gaze flitted away. He saw her swallow and had the feeling he'd just rattled her composure. "All right," he said lightly. "I admit I find the thought of being alone with you rather appealing—very appealing, actually. Though it's not entirely for the reason you think."

Cass stifled a laugh that might have been slightly hysterical if she'd let it escape. With Tyler, she didn't know what to think. She loved the way he teased her, but sometimes she just didn't know when to take him seriously.

"Why, then?" she blurted before she could stop herself.

"Because I've watched you the last few weeks and, lady, you put me to shame. You're constantly on the move from sunup to sundown. I don't think I've seen you sit down for longer than five minutes at a time. Don't you think you deserve to indulge yourself a little?"

He didn't give her a chance to answer. Instead he ran the tip of his finger down her nose. "You seem to think I'm out to spoil Katie. But what I'd really like is to spoil

you for a change." His eyes wandered over her upturned features. "I'll pick you up at eight, okay? And
I'll have you back home no later than midnight, Cinderella."

Cass hesitated, torn despite herself. She couldn't remember the last time she'd had an evening out. Surely
it wouldn't hurt, just this once.

Her slow-growing smile took his breath away. "You
talk a good game, Prince Charming," she told him
lightly. "But remember, not one stroke past midnight,
or I'll see that your fairy godmother turns *you* into a
pumpkin."

He was whistling when he left for home a few minutes later. Cass followed his progress down the sidewalk, feeling faintly troubled. If she didn't watch
herself, she could easily fall head over heels for Tyler.
Rick had never been as sensitive and alive to her needs
as Tyler, even in the early years of their marriage. Nor
could she deny that the female in her thrilled to his caring and concern. But it wouldn't do to let herself get
accustomed to his interest in her.

It wouldn't do at all.

8

TYLER SURPRISED HER by driving them into Milwaukee for dinner. Cass took one look inside the restaurant's dining room and frantically considered bolting in the opposite direction. The atmosphere was subdued but elegant. Gleaming wood panels reflected the flickering glow of candlelight. Crystal glassware and silver cutlery adorned white-linen-covered tabletops. If her hand hadn't been tucked securely beneath Tyler's elbow, anchored there by one of his own, she might have done exactly that.

She bit her lip as the maître d' led them to a secluded table in a corner. When he'd gone, she glanced across at Tyler. "I feed you meat loaf and in return you take me to a place like this?" Nervously, she twisted the gold bracelets circling her wrist. "I think you got the short end of the stick, Tyler."

He just laughed.

When he'd finished his filet mignon a while later, he dropped his napkin onto his plate and beckoned her with a fingertip. Cass leaned closer to catch his whispered words.

"You know what?" His eyes glimmered with amusement. "I think I like meat loaf better."

This time it was Cass who chuckled. "You sound like one of my kids," she teased. "Loyal to the last."

The evening was perfect. Cass found herself wrapped in a rosy haze of pleasure. The food was wonderful and the setting impossibly romantic.

Best of all was the company. They finally had the chance to talk, to get to know one another better, without the risk of being interrupted every few minutes.

She sighed with genuine regret when Tyler asked for the check. Soon they were leaving the city lights behind and speeding toward home. Her eyelids began to droop and she was on the verge of dozing when she felt the car roll to a halt. She snuggled deeper into the seat and smothered a yawn, not bothering to open her eyes. "Are we home already? It seems like we just left."

Her door swung open and she heard a low chuckle. Her eyes popped open to see Tyler standing there. She was startled to see they'd stopped at a viewpoint along the lake, almost directly across from Tyler's house. Beyond his silhouette, gently undulating waves glistened in the moonlight.

Tyler extended a hand to her. "Cinderella didn't get to dance at the ball yet," he reminded her smoothly.

Cass let him pull her from the car and laughed breathlessly. "But there's no mu—"

Before she could finish, he reached over and pressed a button on the tape player. The sound of a slow, sweet love song drifted into the still night air. Without a word he pulled her into his arms.

He smelled of soap and some light woodsy scent that teased her senses. Her pulse quickened; she told herself it was the wine she'd had tonight, but deep inside she knew better. In that moment she was achingly reminded of all she had missed these last few years. Tyler

Grant was very much a man . . . and made her feel very much like a woman. She closed her eyes and let her body be lulled by the easy, swaying motion of his.

His whisper teased her ear. "Did I tell you how nice you look tonight?"

Cass flushed with pleasure. She wore a summery, cream-colored sheath that belted at the waist. A short, matching jacket complemented the camisole-styled bodice, but she'd slipped it off in the car. Gold hoops dangled at her ears.

"So do you," she told him with an unaccustomed shyness. She opened her eyes and let her gaze alight once more on his pin-striped shirt and tan jacket.

"Thank you," he murmured gravely. His eyes holding hers, he guided her right hand to his chest. The pressure of his fingers eased her palm flat against his chest. Before she knew what he was about, he laid claim to her waist and tugged her closer.

Cass felt her mouth go dry. Beneath the soft fabric of his shirt, the raspy crispness of body hair teased her fingertips. The intimate pressure of his thighs bonding with hers infused her breasts with a tingling heaviness. Yet when he tucked her head into the hollow of his shoulder, his jawline pleasantly rough against her temple, the budding feelings inside went beyond the sensual. Cass felt as if she'd come home after a very long journey.

The song ended. Neither seemed willing to forego the heady promise of the other's arms.

Ironically, it was Tyler who pulled away first. "We'd better head back," he murmured, "if I'm going to have you back by midnight."

The ride home was very quiet. Cass didn't protest when he parked in front of her house and walked her to the door. She noted distantly that the living room was dark; Katie had apparently gone to bed.

All at once her heartbeat was sharp and hard and almost painful. She fumbled in her purse for her keys. Pulling them out, her eyes sought Tyler's. "I can't thank you enough for tonight, Tyler. I had a great time, honestly." Her laugh was breathless again. "I'll sleep like a log tonight."

Tyler nearly groaned. He wouldn't sleep at all. Being with her tonight had tied him up in knots. Watching her talk, enjoying the sound of her laughter, had only made him all the more desperate to sample those raspberry-colored lips once more. The satin sheen of her bare shoulders tantalized and aroused him almost past bearing.

Lust? supplied a curious voice in his mind. *Banish the thought and perish the word.* Certainly there was desire. Something else, too, something he'd never felt before and didn't fully comprehend. A kind of protectiveness, a need to take a little of the burden from this woman's shoulders. That was what tempered the pounding need drumming through his veins.

"The ball doesn't have to end at midnight, you know. If you're free, why don't you come over tomorrow afternoon? We could go swimming and spend the rest of the day lazing around, just the two of us."

If you're free . . . just the two of us. Cass cringed inside. Why did they sound like such—such dirty words? It was then that a horrible thought struck her. Maybe she'd been wrong, after all. Tyler had made no bones about wanting to be alone with her tonight. Maybe he wasn't entirely comfortable around her children. Perhaps where Tyler was concerned, her kids were in the way...as they had been, all of them, in the way of Rick's freedom.

Her fingers clutched the cold, hard metal of her keys. "I can't," she said, keeping her voice very low.

He frowned. "Why not?"

Her smile made her feel as if her face would crack into a thousand pieces. "As much as I'd like to, I left the kids alone tonight. I know I sound like a mother hen, but there were some rough spots when their father left and . . ." Too late, she realized what she had almost divulged. "I really think I should spend the day with them."

In that split second Tyler realized his mistake. He wasn't used to the encumbrances and restrictions children placed on parents and experienced a niggling little twinge of guilt. If she'd been any other woman, he wouldn't have thought twice about sweet-talking her into his home and into his bed. What stopped him was that she was different from any other woman he'd known. She was refreshingly honest and direct and . . .

And she had four kids. That alone was enough to make him think twice about deepening his involvement with her. He'd just spent the last few weeks trying very hard not to feel the way he was feeling right now. Only when he was with her, nothing else seemed to matter.

"The solution is obvious, then." Even as he spoke, Tyler wondered if he'd gone crazy. "All of you can come."

Her breath came out as a weary sigh. "Tyler, it's really very nice of you to offer. But you've done too much already. I wouldn't dream of imposing any further—"

"Hold it right there. *Imposing*? I don't care for that word at all. Have I been imposing these last few weeks?"

"No. No, of course not. But there's only one of you and five of us—"

"And the five of you can stay for dinner, too."

That made her smile, though only a second earlier it had been the last thing she'd felt like doing. "You're going to fix dinner?" she asked dryly.

"I haven't come to your classes for nothing," he stated brashly. "Why, thanks to you I have French toast and pancakes down to a fine art. In fact, I'm looking forward to dazzling you with my newly acquired culinary ability."

She was dazzled, all right. But his smile had a lot to do with it.

His eyes had taken on a teasing light. "Or maybe the idea of a whole weekend without having to fix dinner doesn't appeal to you."

Cass felt herself weakening. There was no doubt about it; he *was* determined to spoil her and knew just how to do it. She knew she should refuse, but somehow the words just wouldn't come.

He stepped closer. "Well?" he asked lightly. "Have I convinced you, or do you need a little more persuasion?"

His gaze was avid and warm on her upturned face. Her pulse skittered alarmingly as she breathlessly speculated what form his persuasion might take.

"All right. You win." She gave in with a tiny little laugh.

Tyler's expression conveyed his pleasure. A finger at her chin, he guided her lips to his. His kiss was short and sweet, but it was all he dared.

TODD WENT WILD when he found out Tyler had invited them swimming. One o'clock Sunday afternoon found four small faces waiting impatiently by the door. Cass cast one last, critical glance at her reflection, wishing for the latest in fashionable swimwear instead of her royal-blue maillot that had seen more summer seasons than she cared to remember.

Once they were down by the lake, she felt just a twinge uncomfortable at baring so much skin in front of Tyler. Katie and Todd took care of that in short order, though, ripping the concealing towel from her hips and laughing uproariously.

Tyler, bringing up the rear, was clearly amused. All thoughts of her own scanty attire dissipated when he pulled off his shirt and dropped it onto the sand. The bottom dropped out of her stomach; all she could do was stare.

Her first thought was that he obviously didn't spend all of his time behind a desk. Her second was that she had never before realized how deceiving the restrictions of clothing were. Her third and last thought—for a very long time—was that a man who looked the way he did right now ought to be outlawed.

His body was lean and spare, superbly muscled and proportioned. His limbs were coated with a silky layer of golden-brown hair that grew darker and thicker on his chest and abdomen. Cass couldn't stop her gaze from traveling a forbidden pathway. Her eyes dipped to lower regions and lingered for a heart-stopping moment on swim trunks that covered only the bare necessities.

"Come on, Mom! You have to go in, too!"

"Oh, no!" she protested. But they pushed her into the lapping waves and sent a stinging spray of water coursing over her bare shoulders.

The chill of the water made her gasp. Oh, well, she thought with a giddy laugh. At least they had succeeded in cooling her off. Just looking at Tyler had overheated her.

Ten minutes later she dragged herself from the water, still gasping and laughing. Retreating to the quilt they'd spread on the sand, she collapsed and settled down to watch Tyler in the water with her children. The sun beat down upon her, warming her and stripping away the tension of the past weeks. The sand was like a soft cushion beneath the quilt; the breeze a gentle caress over her skin. Her lids began to droop. Pillowing her head on her hands, she let her eyes float shut.

It wasn't long before she found herself drifting in and out of the nebulous world between sleep and wakefulness. She roused when the tightening of the quilt alerted her to another presence. Thinking it was Katie, whose voice she'd heard a few seconds earlier, she turned her head slightly, but didn't bother opening her eyes.

"Grab some of that sunscreen," she mumbled, "and put it on my back, will you, sweetie?"

Scant seconds later warm, soothing lotion slid over her shoulders. Massaging fingertips began gliding down the length of her back. She realized almost instantly that something wasn't right.... She jerked up onto her elbows.

Her eyes veered to the bottle of sunscreen and back again. The shock on her face was something to behold. Tyler found himself torn between the urge to laugh and the desire to pull her into his arms, regardless of the spectators.

A slow grin crept across his lips. "You did ask," he reminded her. "And I did promise to spoil you..." He leaned forward, his grin positively wicked. "...*sweetie.*" A hand between her shoulder blades, he pushed her gently down again.

It wasn't long before she released a bubbly sigh of contentment. "You know," she murmured drowsily, "this could be habit-forming."

Tyler's hand left her reluctantly. He leaned back on his heels, calmed the ragged tremor of his breathing and stared at her mouth. Yes, he thought. God, yes. Her hair was pulled into a loose topknot, and shiny, errant curls strayed down her neck. He ached with the need to plunge his fingers into her hair and let it tumble over his hands like warm silk. He wanted to turn her over, to mold the entire length of that sweet, supple body against his, and lose himself in the honeyed depths of her mouth.

Unfortunately, there was only one obstacle... or rather, there were four. And one of them chose that precise moment to run up and drop onto the quilt.

"I've had enough water for today," Katie announced cheerfully. "My skin's starting to look like a prune." She began rummaging through the bag. "Hey, I thought you brought shampoo.... Here it is." She bounded to her feet. "I'm gonna go change now."

Cass rolled over, shielding her eyes from the glare. A jolt went through her as she spied Tyler's eyes on her, hotter than the sun. His gaze slid over her, leaving no part of her untouched. At the flare of masculine appreciation she saw on his face, she went hot, then cold, then blazingly hot again.

Her heart fluttered nervously. It was impossible not to be sexually aware of him. The slanting rays of the sun touched his head, highlighting the sun-kissed luster of his hair and turning his skin to bronze. She fought a sudden impulse as she wondered what it would be like to trail her fingertips over the beard-roughened plane of his lean cheeks. Over his mouth with its sensually curved lower lip . . .

Whoa, lady. It's time to come up for air. She caught herself just in time. Her gaze dropped abruptly, but the sight that met her eyes was no less dangerous. Tiny droplets of water glistened like winking diamonds in the dense gold down that covered his chest and the whole of his abdomen. She couldn't decide if she was relieved or disappointed when Todd yelled for Tyler to come back into the water.

Again and again throughout the afternoon she found her eyes straying to Tyler's bare torso. She tried not to think about how wide his shoulders were, how tight the muscles in his arms looked, how it would feel to run her fingers through the mat of hair on his chest.

But she did nothing more strenuous than lift a glass to her lips—and it was heavenly. For dinner Katie and Tyler barbecued hot dogs and hamburgers on the grill. Trisha proudly set a small plate upon the picnic table and turned to her mother.

"I helped, too, Mommy," she boasted. "I peeled the carrot sticks."

Cass quickly slid an arm around her daughter. "You did such a good job, too. I think I'll have one right now."

It ended up being one of the best days Cass had spent in a long, long time. It was after ten o'clock before she and the kids left for home. Trisha had fallen asleep on Tyler's sofa, so he offered to carry her.

Inside her house, Katie disappeared into the bathroom. Worn out from all the activity, Todd yawned and mumbled good-night. Cass escorted a sleepy Samantha down the hall. Tyler trailed along behind her, Trisha's blond head nestled cozily against his shoulder. He lowered Trisha gently to the bed, then tactfully retreated.

Sam had changed into her nightgown and crawled into the top bunk before Cass even had Trisha stripped of her clothes. She had just tucked the sheet and lightweight blanket over the two, when Katie stepped into the room.

"I'm beat, Mom." She pulled back the sheet on her bed. "See you in the morning."

Cass swallowed an unexpected pang. "Katie?"

The girl turned.

Cass stepped forward. "Katie, I—I just wanted to let you know how much I appreciate all you do here at home. You've had to grow up so fast—maybe too fast. I worry sometimes that maybe I take you for granted. But I don't know what I'd have done without you these last couple of years." She smiled shakily and smoothed her daughter's hair. "I love you, honey."

Katie's eyes squeezed shut as they hugged each other. Her voice was suspiciously husky as she whispered, "I love you, too, Mom. You're the best."

Cass watched her slip into bed, then drew the sheet up over her and kissed her cheek. She was at the door when Katie spoke once more. Cass turned, her hand poised just above the light switch.

Katie gestured toward the living room. "He likes you, Mom." Blue eyes sparkled impishly. "He *really* likes you."

Cass watched her daughter closely. "That doesn't bother you, does it." It was more a statement than a question.

For a fraction of a second, the light in Katie's eyes dimmed. "Dad's not coming back, Mom." Her tone was quietly fierce. "We both know he's not *ever* coming back." She glanced at the bunk beds where her sisters slept, then back at her mother. "And Tyler . . . he's an all-right guy. All of us like him."

Cass went very still inside. She had the strangest idea that Katie was giving her the green light, though perhaps Katie didn't even know it herself . . . but for what? To start an affair with her newest neighbor? Cass knew better than to think an affair was what Katie had in mind, and assured herself hastily it was the last thing she was thinking of.

But she also had to be honest with herself. Sex could never be casual with her; sex and commitment went hand in hand. At the very least, a long-term relationship would need to be firmly established before she could even think of sharing herself in that very special way. . . .

She swiftly clamped the brakes on that particular thought. If Tyler thought she was interested in anything other than a nice, placid affair, he'd probably run the other way.

Cass sighed. Affairs. Long-term relationships. Tyler had given her no sign that he wanted either. Why worry over nothing? In the meantime, however, Katie was still waiting expectantly.

She shook her head and smiled. "It looks like the vote is unanimous, then."

"So you like Tyler, too? As much as we do?"

More, she thought helplessly. *Far more....* "Yes," she said softly. "I like Tyler, too."

The conversation was still fresh in her mind when she headed back into the living room. Tyler stood at the window, staring out at the star-studded sky. She paused, seized by an uncertainty that was rare these days and not liking the feeling at all. While she was grateful for everything he had done for them today, all at once she was painfully aware that here they were, just the two of them.

She must have made some slight noise. He turned and smiled at her. "Kids all set for the night?"

She nodded.

"Good." He moved several steps closer, slipping his fingers into the pockets of his slacks. Cass swallowed, aware of a strange curling sensation in the pit of her stomach. His hands were lean and strong-looking, with a generous sprinkling of golden hair across their wide backs.

"Tyler?"

He lifted his brows and waited.

Cass pushed a strand of hair behind her ear, feeling inexplicably shy. "Thanks for asking us to come swimming today. The kids had a great time."

"I'm glad," he said softly. He tipped his head to the side and regarded her. "But what about you?"

TAKE FOUR

BEST SELLER ROMANCES

FREE!

♥

Best Sellers are for the true romantic! These stories are our favourite Romance titles re-published by popular demand.

♥

And to introduce to you this superb series, we'll send you four Best Sellers absolutely FREE when you complete and return this card.

♥

We're so confident that you will enjoy Best Sellers that we'll also reserve a subscription for you to the Mills & Boon Reader Service, which means you could enjoy...

♥

Four new novels
sent direct to you every two months (before they're available in the shops).

Free postage and packing
we pay all the extras.

Free regular Newsletter
packed with special offers, competitions, author news and much, much more.

CLAIM YOUR FREE GIFTS OVERLEAF

Mills & Boon FREE BOOKS CERTIFICATE

YES! Please send me my four FREE Best Sellers together with my FREE gifts. Please also reserve me a special Reader Service subscription. If I decide to subscribe, I shall receive four superb Best Sellers every other month for just £6.40 postage and packing free. If I decide not to subscribe I shall write to you within 10 days. Any FREE books and gifts will remain mine to keep. I understand that I am under no obligation whatsoever - I may cancel or suspend my subscription at any time simply by writing to you. I am over 18 years of age.

9A2B

MS/MRS/MISS/MR _____

ADDRESS _____

_____

POSTCODE _____ SIGNATURE _____

POST TODAY
and we'll send you this
cuddly Teddy Bear.

**PLUS a free
mystery gift!**
we all love mysteries, and
so we've an intriguing gift
especially for you.

MILLS & BOON
FREEPOST
P.O. BOX 236
CROYDON
CR9 9EL

She wished he would stop staring at her. His gaze was unerringly direct, a little too piercing for her to be entirely comfortable with.

Her laugh was a little nervous. "You succeeded in spoiling me, too."

"Good." His voice brimmed with satisfaction. His smile turned her heart over, while the warmth in his eyes made her feel like Silly Putty inside. He surprised her by holding out his hand in silent invitation. She surprised herself by reducing the gap between them with swift and unwavering steps.

His hand closed around hers. He stared at her as if intent on committing every feature to memory. The air around them grew heated. Her heart began to beat with thick, uneven strokes. The fingers of his other hand came up. Gently, oh, so gently, he touched her cheek. His fingers slid down her throat, settled with disturbing accuracy over the frantic throbbing of her heart.

The touch of his mouth, when at last it came, was like a benediction. Soft and sweet, so tender and beguiling that she wanted to cry. She felt bereft when his head slowly lifted.

He rested his forehead against hers. "Would you be angry if I said I've been wanting to do that since last night?"

"No," she whispered. And God help her, it was the truth.

Every nerve in her body was screaming and at attention, but her knees felt like melted butter. She wanted him to kiss her again, she realized. She wanted it so much, she thought she'd die if he didn't.

The sound he uttered was half laugh, half groan. "I hope you mean that, Cass. Lord, but I do." His heart set up a wild stampede, knowing that Cass felt the same. He glimpsed the same heated awareness in her eyes, felt the same chaotic response in the rapid tattoo of her pulse beneath his hand.

His mouth came down once more, claiming hers. She gave a tiny whimper—or did she only imagine it? Trapped in a haze of conflicting emotions, she splayed her hands against his chest, intending to break off the kiss before it deepened further. Instead her body displayed a shocking will of its own; her fingers crept up to cup the back of his neck and stroke the warm skin there.

She had no conscious awareness of moving to the sofa. One minute they were standing, arms entwined, mouths fused together. The next they were lying on the sofa, his body a heavy but welcome weight against hers.

Her mind was spinning, her senses magnified a hundredfold. The chest her hands now rested on was taut and muscular; she could feel again the faint rasp of hair beneath the thin shirt he wore. A pair of hard thighs was wedged tightly against her own.

But it was the undeniably intimate feel of what lay nestled between the binding of those firm, masculine thighs that caught her attention.

He wanted her, she realized. *Tyler wanted her.* Man to woman. Woman to man. She clung to him, afraid of losing the exquisitely painful delight she felt, just as afraid this was all wrong....

Tyler had known that one kiss would never be enough, just as he had known that if he touched her, he wouldn't be able to stop. She was too warm, too sweet, too tempting to resist.

He loved the way her fingers knotted in his hair, her tiny little shiver when his tongue first touched hers. Taking his time, he coaxed and teased, bringing her tongue out of hiding until it danced shyly against his.

Tyler was lost. His hand trespassed beneath the flimsy cotton of her top. He splayed his fingers over her naked ribs, laying claim to the narrow span of her waist. Unable to help himself, his hand deserted the satin warmth of her skin, only to hover just above the buttons of her blouse.

Cass began to tremble. There was a heaviness deep in her belly, a restlessness that wouldn't be denied. She couldn't lie to herself any longer. In some distant part of her mind she sensed that she and Tyler had been heading toward this moment since the first day they had met. He made her come alive with sensations she'd buried long ago. But there was something about him that was dangerous. He made her feel very female... and very vulnerable.

"Tyler." That odd-sounding voice. Was it really hers?

He liked the sound of his name on her lips. He wanted to hear it a hundred other ways. In passion. In hunger.

The first button slid free of its bondage. Then another and another.

Cass clutched his shoulders. Whether she intended to pull him closer or push him away, she didn't know. Heaven help her, she didn't!

"Tyler, I—I don't think we should be doing this."

His lips swallowed her halting whisper. "Why not?" Greedy fingers plied slowly downward.

She thought of her quivering response, the way her body clung shamelessly to his, as if he were all she had ever wanted. It had been so long since she had been

touched like this . . . too long. Yet it was all wrong. . . .
Her mind groped frantically. There had to be a reason;
it hovered just beyond the fringes of awareness.

"Because I . . . I'm a mother with four children in the
house."

He smiled against her lips. "So?"

The edges of her blouse flicked open. Deft fingers
found and located the front clasp of her bra. It took a
tremendous effort to talk, to even breathe. "Tyler," she
said faintly, "this isn't something a mother should be
doing."

His chuckle was husky and did funny things along
her spine. "I think you're forgetting how those four
children got here."

No, she thought frantically. She hadn't, and that was
the whole problem. She knew exactly where this was
leading. . . . But it felt so good, so right. His palms stole
relentlessly upward to close, slowly and possessively,
over both breasts. His thumbs skimmed over and
around each straining peak, a bold and daring manip-
ulation that ended much too soon. Sharp pinwheels of
pleasure burst inside her, a pleasure so intense she almost cried out. *Again,* she prayed helplessly, the budding crests of her breasts achy and tight. *Again . . .*

Tyler felt a purely male thrill when her nipples
peaked against his palm. Her skin was like warm velvet, enough to drive him mad. He wanted to strip away
her clothes, explore every sweet, supple inch of her and
imprint her body with the feel of his.

His kiss was hungry and urgent, but she didn't disappoint him. Her quickening breath echoed in his
mouth. His hands slid down to her waist, his fingers

tightening almost convulsively as he cupped her against his straining hardness for a never-ending moment.

"Mommy?"

The quavering little voice brought them both back to reality with a heart-stopping jolt. Her eyes flew open to meet Tyler's startled gaze. "Oh, my God!" she gasped. "It's Trisha!"

9

SHE PUSHED at his shoulders desperately.

Tyler grimaced and sat up slowly, his body still burning with need. He was annoyed at the interruption—who wouldn't be? A dark stab of humor hit him. Had it come a few minutes later, the timing could have been crucial indeed.

Cass was fumbling with the buttons of her blouse as she jumped up. The oddest thought flitted through Tyler's mind as he heard her run toward Trisha. He had the feeling she was running *away* from him....

He could hear Cass murmuring to Trisha. The little girl's voice had had the effect of dowsing his head in a cold shower, but one particular part of his body was far slower in responding. He shoved his hand through his hair and tried not to think about the full, insistent pressure between his thighs that was only now beginning to subside.

Cass came back into the room, leading Trisha by the hand. "Uh . . . Trisha can't sleep."

I noticed, Tyler thought wryly. He waited for Cass to turn around and lead the little girl back down the hall and back into bed.

It didn't happen.

Instead she slid an arm around Trisha's shoulders. "I'll bet I know what might help. How about some hot chocolate?"

Tyler narrowed his eyes. Cass seemed almost grateful for the presence of her small daughter!

"Cass," he pointed out with a calm he was suddenly far from feeling, "hot chocolate might be fine in the winter. But it's still eighty degrees outside."

"Well, a glass of milk, then. How's that sound, honey?" Her tone was bright—too bright, he decided. And she had yet to meet his eyes. Tyler was suddenly chafing inside. He suspected she wished he would disappear into thin air!

The little girl nodded eagerly. Trisha, he noted grimly, was nobody's fool. Her mother was going to let her stay up, and she was ready to milk the opportunity for all it was worth.

"Tyler, how about you? Would you like something?"

Yes, he wanted to shout. *What I want is you!*

He made his tone clipped and abrupt. "No." He turned and strode from the room, his posture stiff and rigid.

Behind him, Cass bit her lip. She bent and whispered to Trisha to wait for her in the kitchen. She caught up with Tyler just as he reached the front door and quickly slipped in front of him.

"Wait!" she said breathlessly. "Where are you going?"

"Where else? Home." He glared at her. "And don't ask why, because it's patently obvious you want me out, so why not just admit it? You latched on to Trisha like she was heaven-sent!"

His coolness stung. His lips were ominously thin, his eyes cutting. Cass was utterly miserable. God, if he only

knew how much she wanted him to stay! But she was
far more afraid of what might happen if he did.

And sex was something that could never be casual to
a woman like Cass. She'd been brought up to believe
that love and sex went hand in hand; her values were
too strong for her to discard them so easily.

Tyler made a sound of disgust deep in his throat. He
was handling this rather badly, but he was frustrated
and disappointed. Hurt and angry that Cass was so
damned anxious to be rid of him.

She faltered, still uncertain. "Tyler, I...I didn't mean
for this to happen."

"Don't I know it," he muttered, feeling a muscle jump
in his jaw. "What I don't understand is why, Cass. If you
didn't want anything to do with me, why let me touch
you? Sometimes I think you're a little too proud for
your own good! You're so damned determined not to
accept anything from anyone. Did you think I expected it, because you and the kids spent the day at my
house? Pat me on the head," he mocked, "and give the
boy a kiss—"

She blinked. "You wanted a lot more than just a kiss!"

"So what if I did! I'm only human, and up until the
time Trisha came out, your motor was revved up and
running, too, honey."

She didn't need any reminders, thank you very
much. She was angry at him, angry at herself for letting their embrace escalate so quickly. "You're forgetting I have four impressionable children in the house,"
she reminded him stiffly.

"Am I? I'm beginning to think I have to stand in line
and take a number around here!"

Hell. Hell! He broke off when he saw her blanch—only then did he realize what he'd said. He dragged a hand down his face and cursed himself roundly. That hadn't come out the way he'd planned; he hadn't meant for it to come out, period!

But one look at Cass and he saw he'd just made a grave mistake. Her expression was utterly stricken. Then all at once it was as if a mask dropped into place. Her features were cool and remote, her stance coldly dignified.

She opened the door. Her voice was as clipped as his had been earlier. "Good night, Tyler."

Tyler stared at her. Damn! he thought. What had he done? Her features were closed. There would be no reasoning with her, he knew. And what could he say?

It didn't stop him from trying. He stretched out a hand. "Cass," be began, hesitating.

But Cass was beyond listening. It had been a mistake to let Tyler kiss her...to let herself think they could have anything together. She remembered what Rick had said over the phone that last day....

I've got four kids and a wife hanging around my neck, Cass.... The five of you are like a noose that gets tighter and tighter every minute of every day.... I just can't take it anymore....

She had known what he was saying—they were in the way. And now Tyler was here, saying almost the same thing. Oh, the words were different. But she knew what he meant.

To her everlasting shame, hot tears pricked her eyelids. She hated herself for her weakness and quickly turned her face aside, so he wouldn't see. "Please," she said tonelessly. "Just go."

His hand fell back to his side. He walked out without a backward glance.

THE NIGHT LOOMED stark and lonely. Cass lay wide-awake in her bed, staring at the ceiling. Counting the minutes, counting the heartbeats.

Take a number.

Words. They were just words, uttered in the heat of the moment, in the midst of frustration. She tried telling herself they meant nothing, that she didn't care what Tyler thought of her and her family, that the emotion that sat like a stone on her chest was nothing more than anger. But somewhere along the way, the anger gave way to hurt.

She rolled over and clutched the other pillow to her breast. Why? she cried silently. Why did Tyler Grant have to come into her life now, now, when she was finally getting used to being alone?

With a furious cry, she heaved the pillow across the room. God, how she hated this damned king-size bed! She vowed then and there to buy another—even a cot was preferable to this huge, empty bed—as soon as she was able.

The vow brought precious little comfort against the silence of the night. In bitter frustration, she began once more to count the minutes. And the heartbeats....

The harsh peal of the telephone yanked her from a fitful sleep. She groped for the receiver and dragged it to her ear. "Hello?"

A few seconds ticked by before she heard anything. "I'm sorry."

The cobwebs surrounding her brain were instantly wiped away. She jerked upright, taking the twisted sheet with her. "Tyler." Her gaze flitted to the bedside clock. "Tyler, it's 3:00 a.m."

"I know." He sounded as frustrated as she had been earlier. "But I had to talk to you, Cass. I'm sitting here going crazy, cursing myself for every kind of fool there is. First I acted like a teenage kid who couldn't wait to jump in the back seat. And then I followed it up by acting like a four-year-old who had his candy taken away from him."

There was a brief pause. "I guess I was just letting off steam. I knew you were glad Trisha woke up when she did, and I thought you were using her as an excuse, just so you wouldn't have to be alone with me again."

Guilt rose higher in Cass. She definitely wasn't proud of herself, but she *had* been using Trisha as a shield.

"Then I realized you probably thought I was trying to rush you. And then I thought maybe I'd scared you off."

How ironic. Cass didn't know whether to laugh or cry. From the start she had been certain that she and her brood would be the ones to scare *him* off. But in the end it boiled down to only one thing.

If she didn't watch out for her kids, who would?

"Cass." He spoke her name. "I wasn't taking potshots at you *or* the kids, I swear. And the last thing I want is to hurt you. Tell me you know that."

The fervency of his tone made her head spin. But her heart was still battered and bruised. She drew a deep, tremulous breath. "I—I know," she whispered. Hard as she tried, she couldn't disguise the tiny break in her voice.

"Oh, God," he groaned. "You're crying, aren't you?" When she didn't answer, Tyler knew it wasn't because she didn't want to . . . it was because she couldn't.

He shoved his fingers through his hair. "I can't talk to you like this, Cass." His voice conveyed his urgency. "I'm coming over. Do you hear me?" He didn't wait for an answer. He jammed the phone back into its cradle.

He was on Cass's doorstep less than a minute later. She had barely opened the door than he was inside, slamming it shut with his foot.

"Tyler." Her eyes widened. He was barefoot, wearing only a pair of jeans, and they weren't even zipped. "Oh, Tyler, I can't believe you actually ran over here dressed like that. . . . You're crazy."

"Only since I met you," he muttered and pulled her into his arms. It wasn't instinct that prompted the move, but a need that was deep-seated and intense. Tyler didn't fully understand it. He knew only that to deny it was to deny his very self.

The instant his arms closed around her, a sensation that was poignantly sweet grabbed hold of her heart. Cass closed her eyes and savored the sheltering protection of his arms. She knew it wasn't wise to accept Tyler's comfort, to accept anything from him, but the reasons escaped her right now. Unable to help herself, she clung to him, rubbing her cheek against his bare chest, loving the warm male smell of him and the hair-roughened strength of his chest.

"I'm sorry, Cass." The words broke from his lips. "God, I'm sorry."

"You already said that." Her eyes trickled up the tanned column of his neck. She met his gaze hesitantly.

His hands slid around to cup her shoulders. "And I'm saying it again," he told her feelingly.

Her voice was little more than a wisp of air. "It's all right."

A finger at her chin, he tipped her face up to his. "You're not angry because I kissed you? Because I touched you?"

Quiet as his voice was, the intensity of his tone made her knees weak. Her breath fluttered like a candle in the wind. "No," she whispered helplessly.

Something flashed across his face. Triumph? Relief? Cass couldn't be sure.

She held his gaze as long as she could, then slipped from his arms and moved back several steps. Whenever Tyler touched her, her emotions seemed to run away with her. She felt far more in control with a little distance between them.

Unfortunately, her retreat had the unsettling effect of reminding her of her current state of undress. She crossed her arms over her breasts, suddenly rather keenly aware that she wore only a short, cotton nightie and a thin summer robe that scarcely reached mid-thigh.

Tyler frowned when she turned from him, averting her face. His eyes lingered on her profile. Was she embarrassed, after all? Perish the thought. He uttered a silent prayer that his ego hadn't exceeded his hopes. He didn't want Cass to regret what had happened between them. Damn, but he didn't.

"What's wrong?" he asked quietly.

She merely shook her head. Her wobbly smile caught at his heart.

"Tell me."

Cass took a deep breath. "I was just thinking." She wasn't trying to be evasive, but so much had happened today. She could barely sort through the conflict in her heart, the tumult in her mind.

"About tonight?" The question was just a little sharper than he'd intended.

"Yes." She made the admission reluctantly.

"And?" The single word reflected the same wariness she was experiencing.

She linked her hands before her, wishing she could capture the vaguely unsettling feeling inside her and banish it once and for all. "I don't know," she said slowly. "But maybe what happened tonight . . ."

"Shouldn't have?"

She nodded.

Warm, guiding hands captured her shoulders and slowly turned her around. "Why not?"

She finally risked a glance at him. His expression was gently questioning, even tender. His hair was appealingly tousled over his forehead. She had to clench her fingers to stop herself from smoothing it back over his brow.

Instead she swallowed bravely. "I can't deny it's been nice having another adult around these last few weeks. I never expected it, but you're easy to talk to and fun to be with. I—I like you, Tyler. Quite a lot. But I'm afraid it's not as simple as that. . . ." She stopped, wondering if this was coming out right and very much afraid that it wasn't.

He promptly took up where she left off. "But friends don't have the hots for each other, right?"

Her eyes flashed. "I don't appreciate you laughing at me," she said stiffly. "And just for the record, Tyler, relationships don't start in the bedroom for me."

His smile ebbed when he saw the storm building on her face. All pretense of lightness vanished. "Do you think I don't know that?"

His tone was very quiet, his expression searching. Cass drew a deep breath. Lord, how she envied his calm. "Then why are you bothering with me?"

"Now you're the one who's being incredibly obtuse," he chided gently. His eyes dropped to her mouth. "I happen to have one hell of a reaction to you and it definitely isn't platonic."

"Tyler, it's not hard to figure out the kind of relationships you've had before—everything nice and easy and uncomplicated—no strings, no attachments, no commitments." *And no kids,* she added silently.

Tyler hesitated, filled with two very different and conflicting feelings. Her bluntness made him just a little uncomfortable, yet it was one of the things he liked most about her. Unfortunately, he had a pretty good idea where this conversation was headed and wasn't sure he liked it.

"I won't lie and say it isn't true," he stated quietly. "But if it is, it's not because I insisted that's how the game be played. It's just that with me my work always came first, my personal life second." He gave her a long, thorough look. "Make no mistake, Cass. That's the main reason I'm no longer a trader—and one of the reasons I moved here, one of the things I intend to change."

His conviction was both pleasing and disturbing. She knew what he was saying—that he wasn't a carefree pleasure seeker. "But I have the feeling I'm not like anyone you've ever known before."

His mouth turned down. "Like Suzanne, you mean."

"Y-yes." It hurt to say the words aloud, but it had to be done. "Like Suzanne. I'm not chic and sophisticated like she is."

God forbid, he thought. If Cass was anything like Suzanne, he wouldn't be here right now.

There was an uncharacteristic tremor in her voice. "Let's face it, Tyler. I know what happens when two people don't want the same things. I . . . I'm just too different."

Different. She made it sound like a character deficiency. "That doesn't have to be bad," he observed, keeping his voice very low.

"It's probably not good, either."

He watched a shadow flit across her features. Someone—undoubtedly her ex-husband—had burned her rather badly. He felt a brief flare of anger at the man.

His grip on her shoulders tightened. "Believe me, I know what you're trying to say, Cass. You're not interested in a casual, frivolous, dead-end relationship. And neither am I, thank heaven." Despite the lightness of his tone, his eyes were grave.

"Are you trying to say it makes no difference to you that I have four kids? You've been overwhelmed from the start and you know it!"

There was a brief silence. "All right, I admit it," he said finally. "If someone had told me a year ago that I'd be making a pass at a woman with four children, I'd never have believed it." He stopped, finding it difficult to meet her eyes. "But they're good kids, Cass. I'm proud to say I think we all get along very well."

"But you're glad they're someone else's." It slipped out before she could stop it, even as she told herself she should be glad he was being honest with her.

His lips pressed together. "Dammit, Cass, I didn't say that!"

"You didn't have to, either!" She would have wrenched away, but hadn't gone more than a step before his arms closed around her once more. He pulled her against him, flush to his naked chest.

"So what am I supposed to do, Cass?" His breath rushed past her ear. "Forget what happened here tonight? I hate to tell you this, but I'm not sure that's possible. I can't turn my feelings off and on as easily as all that, and I doubt you can, either."

She couldn't, and had never been more aware of it than at this moment.

Her vision clouded. If she were wise, she'd call a halt to this before it progressed any further. Instead she closed her hands around his muscular forearms, loving the feel of the crisp, golden hair beneath her palms. Weakened by her own treacherous longing, she was unable to summon the words that would send him back where he belonged.

"Tyler," she said shakily. "I wasn't expecting what happened tonight. Maybe I should have, but I didn't." She turned and glanced up at him. "My kids no longer have a father. I no longer have a husband. But I'm coping with single parenthood a lot better than I ever expected, and our lives are finally stable again. There's a little voice inside that tells me I don't need any further complications."

"By that you mean complications of the male variety?"

"Especially the male variety."

Her smile tugged at his heartstrings. Seeing her like this, her hair tumbled over her shoulders, her skin fresh and natural and devoid of makeup, she looked scarcely older than a child herself. She roused feelings in him that were both protective and possessive.

She was so damned vulnerable, he thought, half angry, half frustrated. But she would never have admitted it.

The finger at her chin dictated that she look at him. "Straight from the hip, lady. Do you want me to steer clear of you?"

Cass quivered inside. Why did he have to ask her that straight out? She couldn't say yes; she couldn't say no. Her resolve crumbled, as if it had never existed.

She shook her head, helpless. Tyler Grant, with his suave, easy charm, had somehow managed to invade her sane, practical existence and leave her emotions in a shambles. "To tell you the truth I—I'm not sure how I feel or what I want. All I know is that I don't dare let myself plunge headfirst into something I might regret later."

Oddly, he understood, if only because his entire being had been in chaos since that very first day. Cass wasn't certain she was willing to risk any involvement with him or any other man.

But weren't they already involved? And hadn't tonight proved that beyond a doubt?

The voice of reason resounded in his brain. He told himself she was right. They *were* very different, and Cass Lawrence would not be an easy woman to walk away from. Besides, a little breather would give him a chance to think about his improbable fixation upon his lovely neighbor.

Nonetheless, he couldn't quite banish a twinge of regret.

"I understand perfectly," he acknowledged with a faint lift of his brows. "From now on, it's hands off. No steamrolling tactics whatsoever."

Cass peered at him uncertainly. She wasn't sure if she was disappointed or relieved. "You don't mind?"

"Not at all. I do have one request, though."

She tried to match his bantering tone. "And what might that be?"

Their eyes locked. A dozen wordless messages echoed between them, messages neither could deny or express. It was illogical—irrational, she concluded. But the sudden blaze that flared in his eyes thrilled her clear to the tips of her toes.

He reached for her.

Her common sense hadn't deserted her, after all. She tried to step back, but he caught her by the shoulders. Her hands came up to his chest.

"Tyler, wait." Her protest was as faint as her resistance. "I thought you just said . . ."

"You wouldn't deny a starving man his last meal, would you?"

Cass bit her lip to keep from laughing. "This isn't funny."

"I know," he whispered.

Despite her vow, despite his, their lips met and clung.

It was a kiss that sent her spinning away to a magic place, made all the more so because she didn't believe in magic. Once, long ago, she had believed in romance, in love everlasting, but Rick's betrayal had pried her eyes wide open.

But she couldn't stop her hands from curling around his shoulders, her fingers from twining into the golden roughness of the hair that grew low on his nape.

They were both breathing rapidly when Tyler finally lifted his head. "Oh, Cass." Her name was half laugh, half groan. "You know you aren't making it easy for me to leave here." One more kiss, then he forced himself to say good-night and head for home.

He could still feel the imprint of her body molded against his when he climbed back into bed for the second time that night. His blood was so hot, he felt he was steaming. He reminded himself that his limits had been set, the boundary lines firmly marked and in place. That meant he was going to have to play by the rules.... He was about to discover it was easier said than done.

10

"MOM!" Todd howled. "You put my white sock with my blue one! And yesterday I found a black one with a red one!" He gazed at her accusingly.

"That's nothing," Samantha announced with a giggle. "She put salt in the sugar bowl, and Trisha put it on her cereal this morning."

Katie's eyes gleamed. "Last night when she made popcorn, she forgot to put the lid on the pan. You should have seen her face when she turned around and saw popcorn popping all over the stove and the floor!"

"Very funny," Cass said dryly. "Just for that you get to put these away." She handed her oldest daughter a neatly folded pile of laundry.

"Check my socks!" Todd yelled after Katie.

His grin became a howl when his mother stuck a broom into his hand. "You get to sweep the kitchen floor."

Such conversations had become rather familiar the last few weeks. The kids clearly thought it hilarious that she was so absentminded, but Cass found it rather embarrassing. Unfortunately, she didn't have to wonder why. The reason was easy to find—Tyler Grant . . . a name that was now a household word.

Ever since the night of their sizzling embrace, she had been trying doubly hard to make certain the kids didn't make pests of themselves where Tyler was concerned.

But fate had taken an invisible hand and appeared to be binding their lives together.

She couldn't count the times the two of them had sat on his porch together after the kids were in bed. Sometimes she was wired from a particularly hectic day of baby-sitting. Tyler always knew what to say to make her laugh and ease her tension; he was far more alive and sensitive to her needs than Rick had ever been. And the kids were always thrilled whenever he asked them over to swim.

Then there was the way he showed up nearly every evening for Sam to take Missy for a walk, and as usual, in time to lend a hand with the dishes! Somehow Sam ended up not only with Missy in tow, but her mother and Tyler, as well.

He'd reached hero status in their eyes, all of them. As for Cass, she was both touched and vexed by his growing rapport with her children. Did he think he had to be nice to her kids to make points with her? And why was he trying?

For the first time in quite a while, Cass found herself floundering. He kept her off balance. Light and teasing one minute, the next his gaze was that of a lover, caressing and possessive, communicating private messages filled with stark, sensual wanting. She hadn't imagined she could feel so much heat, just from the silent stroking of his eyes. Yet several times she'd caught him staring at her when he'd apparently thought she wasn't looking, and she'd had the strangest feeling he was just as confused as she was.

She told herself over and over that any involvement with him would be utterly foolish, possibly even disastrous. After what had happened with Rick, she wasn't about to rush into any man's arms, no matter how tempting those arms were. She wasn't thinking only of herself; the kids adored Tyler, too. They all had too much to lose for her to indulge in what could end up as little more than a fling.

But in spite of everything she was still a woman, with the same needs and desires as any other.

Her body was telling her it had been too long since those needs had been fulfilled. It was as if she were starved for closeness, for the touch of a man's hands . . . Tyler's hands. He had only to walk within a few feet of her and she felt all jittery inside. Hours passed before the restless stirrings subsided. Wanted or unwanted, her involuntary reaction to this man worried her.

Even though they kept their distance physically, the emotional bond between them was growing. They talked and laughed with an easy familiarity, as if they had known each other for years.

But his attraction to her confounded her. He had admitted she was different. But the newness would wear off. The charm would wear thin. He might be interested in playing stud to someone he perceived as sex-starved, but playing father to her four children was undoubtedly another story. How long before he felt the kids were in the way. . .as they had been in Rick's? Then where would she be?

The thought made her wince. She tried telling herself that he was just a man like any other—but he wasn't. And one thing was becoming increasingly clear, something that was both frightening and secretly thrilling. Tyler made her feel more like a woman than a mother.

She couldn't rid herself of the notion that it might prove to be her downfall.

CASS WASN'T THE ONLY ONE treading carefully these days. Tyler felt as if he'd been hit on the head. It was just as he'd told Cass. A year ago falling for a woman with four kids had been unthinkable; now it seemed she was *all* he thought about. She filled his mind so thoroughly that for the first time in his life, he was having one hell of a time keeping his mind on his work.

He knew she thought they were the original odd couple, that they were all wrong for each other, and any serious relationship between them was out of the question. In his rational mind he knew she was right.

But the reasons why—and why not—were beginning to matter less and less.

His feelings for her grew stronger with each day. In all honesty, Tyler couldn't think when he'd admired anyone more. To him, the task she'd assumed of taking on four children beside her own was mind-boggling. But Cass was patient and warm and loving, no matter what; it showed in the way she slid an arm around Sara and Dave. Brian, he had discovered, could be a little hell-raiser at times. But Tyler liked the way Cass handled the boy. She was calm and firm and always fair when mediating the squabbles he and Todd occasionally had. And he loved the lilting way she laughed when Emily flung chubby arms around her neck and puckered up for a kiss.

He thought of Cass by day... and longed for her by night.

The second week in August turned blazingly hot and sultry, with temperatures in the midnineties, and the humidity lagging only slightly behind. Despite the heat he decided to mow his lawn. Maybe a little honest sweat and exercise would purge his torrid state of mind. His dreams had lately gone from smoldering to scorching.

He had just finished when he heard several voices hailing him. Shielding his eyes against the glare of the sun, he saw that Todd, Samantha and Trisha had set up their lemonade stand in their driveway. Their diligent efforts hadn't waned at all in the last weeks. He'd been a little surprised when Trisha proudly displayed their treasury one day, a peanut butter jar stuffed with change and dollar bills.

They were all smiles when he ambled their way.

"We've got pink lemonade today," a beaming Trisha informed him.

"You're just in time," added her brother. "I just put a whole tray of ice cubes in it, so it's real cold."

Sam gazed up at him hopefully. "You want some, don't you?"

He swiped his hand across his forehead in an exaggerated motion. "Well," he said with a grin, "looks like you've snagged your first customer of the day." He dug into his pocket and started to hand Todd a dime.

The boy pointed to the sign he'd just taped to the front of the table. "We're charging a quarter now," he said with a sheepish grin. "It's so hot we figure we'll sell more—especially on a Saturday, when everybody's working outside like you. And that way we'll make more money."

"So I see." Tyler hiked an eyebrow and passed him another nickel and dime. "Todd, my boy, you may have a future in finance, after all."

Hoping that Cass might spy him lingering outside, he stayed and chatted with the three while he drank his lemonade. Trisha looked at him curiously. "When's your birthday?"

"It's funny you should ask," he said, smiling. "Because my birthday happens to be next Saturday."

"Really?" Todd and Samantha exchanged glances, while Trisha clapped her hands. "Mommy always makes us a birthday cake."

Sam's eyes lighted up. "Yeah. It's sorta like chocolate—"

"It's called red velvet cake," Todd supplied. "And boy, is it good!"

Red velvet. Tyler nearly groaned. The words inspired wild and rampant visions of Cass's lips.

"Sounds fantastic," he murmured, tearing his mind away from Cass. Considering the fact that he was in the presence of three of her children, it seemed almost lascivious to think of her in that way. "To tell you the truth," he mused, "I can't even remember the last time anyone made me a birthday cake. It was probably before I left home for college."

Lost in thought, he didn't see Todd and Sam exchange glances. Sam excused herself and ran off toward the house.

Trisha tipped her head to one side. "How old you gonna be?" she demanded.

"Thirty-six." His smile widened when her eyes grew round.

"That's even older than Mom," Todd put in. "She's only thirty-four."

"You make it sound as if I'm ancient." Tyler chuckled. "Your dad must be about the same age, isn't he?"

He wasn't prepared for the flat silence that followed. Todd's expression grew rather uncomfortable. His gaze slowly fell; he fidgeted nervously with the pile of paper cups on the tray. "I don't remember how old my dad is," he said finally. "I—I better go get some more cups."

He dashed off before Tyler could say another word. Tyler followed the boy's progress into the house. He couldn't help but think that Todd's reaction was very much like Cass's had been, the day he'd brought up the subject of child support. Trisha, however, was unperturbed. She grinned up at him, swinging her legs beneath her chair.

"Trisha." Tyler hesitated, glad that no one else was here, yet guilty that he felt that way. "Don't you kids ever see your father?"

It wasn't the first time he'd pondered the question. It was only logical to assume their father would have custody at least a weekend a month, some kind of visitation rights. But nearly two months had passed, and Tyler was certain that their father had yet to make an appearance. It was odd, he thought. Very odd.

His conviction doubled when Trisha shook her head.

He knelt so he was on the same level with her. "Does your dad live somewhere else?" he asked gently. "Maybe in another state? A city other than Crystal Lake?"

Again she shook her head.

"But doesn't he at least send birthday presents? Christmas gifts to the four of you?"

Her face fell. Tyler cursed himself and wished he hadn't asked.

Trisha looked at him earnestly. "My daddy ran off a long time ago," she confided in a small voice. "We don't know where he is. Nobody does."

Tyler balked. Ran off? Was that Trisha's choice of words or someone else's? He strongly suspected the latter. It wasn't until he noticed her watching him solemnly, her blond brows puckered in a slight frown so like her mother's, that some nameless emotion squeezed his heart.

He summoned a smile, reached out and tweaked a blond pigtail. "Hey, you know what? I could sure use another glass of that lemonade."

He was relieved when her expression brightened, but his mind raced on. He'd already suspected that Cass's divorce had been anything but ordinary. Her reluctance to talk about her ex told the story only too well. There was no child support. No visitation. And now this....

Something wasn't right. Tyler was more certain of it than ever. He wanted nothing more than to ask Cass about her ex-husband. But he didn't press when he saw her again, because he sensed that despite her fire, despite her spirit, she was very, very vulnerable. Most of all he wanted her to trust him enough to tell him the whole story.

Tyler didn't know why that should matter so much. But it did. Damn, but it did.

THE FOLLOWING Saturday afternoon, Cass found herself booted out of her own kitchen by four autocratic young people and ordered not to return until she was told to. "What am I supposed to do?" she demanded, laughing.

Katie's head peeked around the doorjamb. "Why don't you go pay Tyler a visit, like he's always asking you to?"

"He's gonna take Missy to the vegetarian," Trisha announced. "Maybe you can help him."

Todd hooted. "The vegetarian? You mean the veterinarian."

Trisha glowered at her brother. "That's what I said."

As it happened, Tyler had no qualms about Cass tagging along while he took Missy to the vet's. She phoned Katie from there to tell her she'd pick up some hamburgers on the way home and heard a lot of laughing and giggling in the background. She was half afraid she'd find her house a disaster area.

But once they were home, the kids still wouldn't let her into the kitchen—or Tyler, either. They ate outside on the picnic table, but then all dashed inside, with strict orders to the two adults to stay put. She and Tyler sat down on the patio to await their summons.

It wasn't long before the sound of running footsteps reverberated inside the house. Tyler's brows rose a fraction. "I think we're about to find out what's behind door number three."

Todd threw open the door, grinning from ear to ear. "You can come in now." The three youngest swarmed around Tyler as he stepped inside. Trisha latched onto his hand and practically dragged him across the floor. Cass trailed behind, trying very hard not to think about the dreadful state her kitchen must be in by now.

That wasn't the case at all. She stopped abruptly and stared in amazement. There in the middle of the kitchen table sat a small, round cake.

"Well..." Cass knew she sounded rather stunned. She turned to the man beside her. "It must be your birthday, because I know it's not mine."

Tyler said nothing. He looked as if he'd been hit over the head. All at once the kids began to speak.

"Do you like it?"

"We baked it all by ourselves!"

"I helped frost it!"

"And I put the candles on!"

Tyler stood stock-still, his gaze still riveted to the cake. One side was higher than the other, the frosting looked as if an army troop had decided a sampling was in order, and the candles weaved a meandering path around the edges.

It was the most beautiful cake he'd ever seen in his life—and so he said.

Four pair of eyes beamed back at him. Tyler swallowed, his throat unexpectedly tight as he hugged each child in turn. When his gaze finally shifted to Cass, he grinned crookedly. "I can't believe they did this."

Cass smiled. He was touched, and man enough not to care if he showed it. Maybe it was only motherly pride, but his reaction warmed her heart.

He rubbed his hands together with relish. "Who wants to cut the first piece?"

Cass laid a knife upon the table. "You're the birthday boy, so you get to do the honors."

"Wait!" Trisha cried. "You didn't blow out the candles yet! Sam helped me put 'em on—all thirty-six of 'em!" She looked crushed at the very idea that he might forego such a tradition.

It appeared Tyler had no intention of disappointing her.

Katie handed her mother the matches. "Hmm," Cass said with a grin. "We'll have to make sure the house doesn't catch on fire before we get all these candles lit." She lighted a match and gave it to him, so he could start on the other side of the cake.

He fixed her with a mock glare. "I'll get you for that one," he promised, "when *your* birthday rolls around."

She wrinkled her nose. "You don't even know when that is."

"True." His mouth quirked as his gaze slid back over his shoulder toward the four children. "But I'll bet I won't have a hard time finding out."

He had a point, Cass conceded with a chuckle. The kids all cheered when he blew out the candles, but one flickered and remained alight.

Samantha looked at him impishly. "One candle left. That means you've got one girlfriend!"

Five pairs of eyes slid unerringly to Cass, whose face stung with the heat of embarrassment. She gave them all a lopsided smile and reached for the stack of plates Katie had set out.

But she widened her eyes when Tyler cut the first piece of cake and slid it onto the plate she held out. "My Lord!" she gasped. "What kind of cake is this?"

"It's red velvet," Sam said hastily. "We used your recipe, Mom. And we followed it exactly."

Katie bit her lip. "Except for the food coloring."

"The food coloring?" Cass's voice was weak.

"We didn't have a bottle of the red stuff," Todd explained. "But we had some green. And a little blue and yellow..."

"So we used all of 'em," Trisha put in happily. "I think it's pretty."

Pretty was not how Cass would have described it. She was half-afraid to speculate on Tyler's reaction, but when she discovered him wearing a silly grin, she found herself relaxing. Neither he nor the kids seemed to mind eating moss-colored cake; Cass hastily swallowed a few bites, trying hard not to think about what she was eating. The kids were jabbering as usual, so she hurriedly carried her plate to the sink and surreptitiously stuffed its contents into the disposal.

As always, Tyler could scarcely take his eyes off her. Green or no, the cake was good. But he might as well have been eating sawdust for all the notice he took of it. His whole being was focused on the woman who had invaded every corner of his life. Tyler couldn't remember a time in the last ten years when he'd been so relaxed and felt so at ease.

In the midst of it all came a phone call. The three youngest whooped wildly when Cass told them her parents wanted to take them along to a friend's lakeshore cabin in northern Wisconsin the next weekend.

Tyler sat very still. With the kids gone, it would be just the two of them. . . . The realization was enough to send his blood pressure skyrocketing. There was a burning heat in his eyes as he tracked her movements. As always, she drove him to distraction. Her hair was swept back from her face and skimmed her bare shoulders whenever she turned her head. Tyler wanted to slide his fingers through it and bury his face in the honeyed strands.

As a concession to the hot weather, she wore white shorts and a loosely fashioned tank top. Her skin had the same downy texture of the ripe peaches that filled the bowl on the counter. The sinewy length of her tanned legs severely tested his control. He dreamed nightly of those long legs wrapped around his hips in the heat of passion.

Watching her move around the kitchen, he chafed at his self-imposed restrictions. He couldn't be with her without wanting to touch her. He wanted to carry her off to bed, to kiss away all the protests he was sure would follow, and make love to her until nothing else mattered. It wasn't just sex, though he wasn't sure Cass would see things that way.

Pushing himself away from the table, he carried his plate to the sink. He paused and glanced back. "I still can't believe those four baked a cake all by themselves," he said with a smile. His gaze drifted to Cass. "If I were you, I'd be proud of them."

Cass felt her heart melt. "Thanks," she said softly. Did he have any idea how his praise warmed her? Their eyes met and held for the longest moment, but once again she found herself reluctant to be pulled into deeper waters.

She lifted her eyes heavenward and commented dryly, "But you'll notice they're rather good at disappearing one by one the minute it's time to wash dishes."

"It's a good thing I'm here, then."

"Well," she said lightly, "you certainly are proving to be indispensable."

Tyler uttered a silent prayer. He hoped so. Lord, but he hoped so.

Even as she said the words, Cass felt an odd tug at her heartstrings. Having Tyler around this summer had been . . . wonderful. But she didn't need a knight in shining armor. She needed . . . what? She was proud of her independence, of her ability to make a life for herself and the kids without benefit of a husband. But sometimes it was oh, so lonely.

She needed someone to hold her. Someone to touch her. Someone to love her.

Where did Tyler fit in? She hated to confront the question, because she didn't have an answer. He was here now. But what about tomorrow? Next year? It was almost a certainty he wouldn't be around forever.

"Why did you quit your job in Chicago?" she asked impulsively.

To her surprise he laughed. "Where on earth did that question come from?"

Cass stared at the mound of suds filling the sink, but suddenly all she could hear was Rick's voice. *I'm tired, Cass. I'm tired of being responsible for a home, a wife and four kids.* She reached over and slowly shut off the faucet.

She chose her words carefully, hoping—praying— she gave nothing away. "I guess I still don't understand why someone would leave a perfectly good job." She took a deep breath. "Especially one like yours. I've heard traders make big money."

"They also lose big money, too. But that's one of the things that tend to get pushed aside. People like you don't hear about the broken marriages, the hard drinking, the nervous breakdowns that are just as much a part of the trading world as the numbers games." His expression grew sober. "I guess you have to be a part of it to fully appreciate the pressure and stress."

Her hands swirled gently in the soapy water. "But you worked at it for quite a while, didn't you?"

"Ten years."

She frowned. "There must have been something that kept you in it all that time."

He took the dish she handed him. "Oh, I can't deny it's fascinating. At times almost addictive. It wasn't until the last year I was there that I realized I was burned-out."

His smile was grim. "Or maybe I was just tired—tired of the rat race. Tired of coming home with my ears still ringing from all the shouting on the floor, tired of being so tense it took hours before I could relax enough to sleep. I used to lie awake at night, thinking about the future, about what I wanted." *And now I lie awake and think about you.*

He paused. "I had everything I ever wanted, or so I thought. Money. Success. But I also paid the price, because there was never a moment to call my own." He gestured vaguely. "I just wasn't satisfied anymore. I finally woke up and realized that what I had just wasn't what I wanted. My boss thought I was kidding when I walked in his office later that morning and told him I wouldn't be back."

Cass's mind veered once more, inevitably, to Rick. It was all she could do to stop from wincing visibly. "So you quit," she said slowly. "Just like that." She was silent a few seconds. "I don't think I could ever be that impetuous."

He watched her, a slight smile on his face. "You call it impetuous," he said gently. "I call it decisive."

"You see?" She tried, but couldn't return his smile. "That just goes to show how different we are."

He tipped his head to the side. "Are we?" he murmured. "I don't think so, Cass. I don't think so at all."

"But Crystal Lake is a far cry from Chicago." The words emerged with difficulty. "Do you think you'll ever go back?"

He chuckled. "You're looking at a man whose work has been nearly his sole existence for almost half of his life. I'm certainly not ready for retirement yet, but I like being my own boss. And I can't imagine ever missing the pressure and the stress."

His answer was all she wanted to hear, all she *needed* to hear. Yet Cass couldn't quite banish the doubt that cast its shadow upon her.

Tyler frowned when he glimpsed her expression. He longed to reach over and smooth the tiny lines etched between her brows, but he'd promised himself he wouldn't lay a finger on her until it was what she wanted, too.

He deliberately made his voice teasing. "Would you miss me if I left?"

Yes, she thought. God, yes. She swallowed and forced herself to match his bantering tone. "Why, of course," she said, looking over her shoulder to see him sliding plates and cups into the cupboard. "I'd have to dry the dishes myself."

"Aha!" His eyes gleamed. "Does that mean I've finally succeeded in spoiling you?"

Oh, Tyler, she thought with a pang. *You've done far more than spoil me. . . .*

She couldn't quite suppress her disappointment when he announced his intention to head home. At the door, Sam gazed up at him mournfully. "I'm sorry we don't have a present for you."

Tyler's expression softened as he glanced at the four small faces. But before he could say a word, Katie offered an apologetic smile. "We didn't think of it until yesterday."

Todd looked embarrassed. "We couldn't figure out what to get you, either. And we wanted to surprise Mom, too."

Trisha's face brightened. "I've got some chocolate kisses in my room."

There was an odd tightening in Tyler's chest. "Now that sounds great," he said with a slow-growing grin. "But to tell you the truth, I'd much rather have the real thing—and maybe even a hug." He tapped his lean cheek. "Feel free to plant one right there," he invited them.

Katie's gaze sped to her mother. Laughter bubbled in her voice. "Even Mom?"

Even Mom, Tyler thought fervently. *Especially Mom.* He pointed to the spot directly in front of him. "Line up right there, ladies. And of course, you, too, Todd."

The girls giggled and obediently stood in a row to hug Tyler and press a kiss upon his cheek. Todd settled for a handshake, then turned beet red when Tyler dropped an arm around his shoulders and pulled him close for a fraction of a second.

The tug on Cass's heart was part pleasure, part pain. It was impossible to remain unmoved by the warm affection that existed between the five of them. She had been so busy trying to put their lives back together again that she had rarely let herself wonder how the lack of a father figure might affect her children.

She did so now. It hurt to acknowledge that perhaps the kids might end up hurt because they no longer had a father.

The thought was cut short when eight small hands prodded her in the back. "Your turn, Mom!" someone said happily.

Cass had no time to protest. She found herself face-to-face with Tyler, staring straight into golden eyes alight with humor—and with something else—something that caused her heart to knock wildly in her chest.

A half grin flirted at the corners of his mouth. "Don't be shy now, Cass," he murmured. "And remember it *is* my birthday."

They stood perilously close. His arms were crossed, his fingers curled around biceps that she knew were as hard and tight as they looked.

The heat that surged through her had nothing to do with the warm summer night. Tyler had such strong, wonderfully masculine hands. Her breasts grew heavy and tight as she remembered how his lean fingers had teased her nipples to quivering erectness.

Her tongue darted nervously around her lips, but Tyler was in seventh heaven as she levered herself up on tiptoe, her hips hovering tantalizingly close to his.

At the last instant he moved, so that her lips brushed his instead of his cheek. Their mouths met and clung for but a moment; it was a kiss that was brief and feather-light, but it sent shivers clear to her toes.

It wasn't enough for either of them . . . and they both knew it.

Cass felt troubled as she followed his progress down the sidewalk a minute later. Their earlier conversation lingered in her mind.

How long would Tyler be satisfied here in Crystal Lake? How long before he yearned for the excitement he'd left behind in Chicago? How long before he packed up and left? Tyler had quit his job almost as if it were a whim—exactly as Rick had done. She couldn't ignore the niggling little voice that reminded her Rick had walked out on his family and responsibilities on the spur of the moment and never looked back.

She was falling hard and fast for a man who might well do the same, and there didn't seem to be a thing she could do to stop herself. Somehow she was going to *have* to.

And soon.

ONE WEEK LATER, Tyler peered out his front window. He felt like a nosy old busybody, but he couldn't help it. He had seen Trisha, Sam, Todd and Katie leave an hour earlier with Cass's parents.

He and Cass had been warily circling each other for the last few days. The temperature shot up another ten degrees whenever they were anywhere near each other. Tyler was slowly going out of his mind, wanting nothing more than to pull her into his arms and mold the entire sweet length of her against him. But he'd promised he wouldn't touch her and he wouldn't—until she gave him some signal that she wanted otherwise.

Hers wasn't a touch-me-not attitude, which didn't make his problem any easier. He wondered grimly if she knew he recognized the silent yearning in her eyes, if only because his own was just as intense.

Ever since that night when Trisha had walked in on them and he'd learned that she was afraid of being hurt—of her kids being hurt—he'd had the feeling she was using her four children as a shield. She was sensitive, protective, and even a little defensive where her kids were concerned.

He suspected it was all connected with her divorce. Nor could he shake the feeling that her ex-husband— not the kids—constituted the real obstacle between them.

It didn't take him long to decide to put his theory to the test. This could be just the opening he'd been looking for, he thought, punching out Cass's phone number.

She picked up the phone on the first ring.

"Hi," he greeted her. "Did I catch you in the middle of something?"

"Please do," she said dryly. "I was just about to make out my grocery list."

"Sounds rather quiet," he commented.

She laughed. "That's what I was thinking—it's *too* quiet and I'm not used to it."

"Why's that?" Somehow he managed to keep the anxiety from his voice. He mentally crossed his fingers. "Because the kids are gone until Monday?"

There was a fractional hesitation. "Yes, and you know what? It's rather lonely here."

She held her breath, wondering if she had just made the biggest mistake of her life.

He held his breath, wondering if his prayers had just been answered.

"If you're looking for company, you don't have to look far. In fact, I could use some company myself, to help me celebrate."

Cass was almost afraid to ask. "What would we be celebrating?"

"I just took the first issue of my newsletter to the printer this afternoon."

"You did? That's great."

"Why don't you come and tell me in person?" When she hesitated, his voice grew very low. "Please, Cass."

Please. He was probably the only man on earth who could make such a simple request sound sexy as hell, without even trying. Cass couldn't refuse . . . and she didn't.

Five minutes later she stepped into Tyler's house. She felt a little shy and awkward without having one of the kids along. Her heart fluttered when he ran an approving eye over her tan slacks and light cotton sweater. She was glad she'd taken the time to change.

He laughed when he saw her tentative expression. "Don't look like that. You've visited the lion's den before and you've always emerged unscathed."

"But usually with four little cubs running around, if not here, then right next door," she reminded him. "I know it's probably silly, but without any of the kids here I feel as if some vital part of me is missing."

I know the feeling, Tyler thought with a pang. *I do, indeed*.

"Why don't we go out back and walk by the lake?" he suggested.

Her laugh was a trifle nervous as she followed him toward the rear of the house. "Hey, you promised champagne, remember? Or do you have ulterior motives, after all?"

"Several," he said without hesitating. He gave her an exaggerated leer as he opened the door and let her pass by. "After all, it's just the two of us, Cass. I have you all to myself."

She found herself relaxing, but only slightly. "Maybe we should talk specifics here."

He stepped onto the deck behind her. "Well," he said lightly, "first I thought we'd do some heavy-duty talking."

Cass stopped so suddenly he barreled right into her. She turned to stare at him. Talking was safe enough, wasn't it? Yet gentle as his tone was, his gaze was probing—a little too probing.

She linked her hands before her and glanced at him. "What did you want to talk about?"

Whether she knew it or not, there was an undercurrent of suspicion lacing her voice. Tyler sighed inwardly. She wasn't going to make this easy for either of them.

He smiled directly into wary blue eyes. "How about you?"

She blinked. That beautiful mouth he so loved straightened into a thin line. "Why can't we talk about you?"

"Because we've done that."

"We've talked about me, too. And every member of my family, if you'll recall!"

But he was already shaking his head. "Have we?" Soft though his voice was, there was a resoluteness to his expression that didn't go unnoticed by the woman before him. "You're forgetting, Cass, that somehow we failed to discuss one very important subject—or maybe I should say two. Your ex-husband and your divorce."

"Didn't it ever occur to you I might not want to talk about either?"

"It has, which is why I haven't pressed the issue." When she would have spun about, he caught her by the arm and pulled her firmly back to face him. He could almost feel her receding into herself, but this time he wasn't going to let her.

"Cass," he murmured, and the gentleness in his voice wrenched at her heart. "I'd like to believe you can tell me anything. I feel that way with you, and it hurts to know you don't feel the same."

Her eyes moved slowly, inevitably, to his. "I do," she whispered helplessly.

"Then talk to me," he urged softly. "Tell me about your husband."

To her horror, there was a huge lump in her throat. She shook her head, unable to do more.

"I don't want this to be difficult for you, Cass, so I'll try to make it as painless as possible." He swallowed, wishing there were another way to say this, but knowing there wasn't. For Cass's sake he prayed he was wrong. Yet if he was, he'd only succeed in well and truly jamming his foot into his mouth.

He paused for the space of a heartbeat. "Did your husband desert you?"

11

THERE WAS AN AGONY of silence. One look at her stricken expression was all it took for Tyler to realize he was right.

He almost wished he had said nothing. Almost... but not quite.

His hand came up in a tentative gesture. His touch immeasurably gentle, he tucked a strand of honey-gold hair behind her ear. She tensed, but didn't draw back as he'd expected.

To her horror Cass heard her voice tremble. "How did you know?"

Tyler saw her convulsive swallow and knew the question cost her no small price. When he finally spoke, his voice was very low.

"When you told me there was no child support, I think I knew then that something was wrong. And then I kept waiting for someone to come around and take the kids for a weekend. But that never happened. Then last week, Trisha said that her daddy· -" he hesitated "—that he ran off. And the more I thought about it, the more I decided it could mean only one thing—that he deserted you."

He wasn't prepared for the pain that splintered her features. Seeing it, Tyler's hand reached instinctively for hers. Her skin was icy cold. He tenderly imprisoned her hand within both of his, praying he could make this easier, yet knowing he couldn't.

He hated himself when she turned her face aside. Her shoulders slumped. Her eyes closed, her chin dipped, and a dozen different emotions twisted his heart.

"Cass, don't." His voice was as raw as hers had been. "Don't be ashamed. Don't be embarrassed. I don't know why he left, but I know it couldn't have been your fault, so don't blame yourself."

Don't blame yourself. Even as Cass floundered, feeling naked and exposed, she marveled that Tyler knew her so well. The moment wasn't as awkward as she'd feared. When she finally found the courage to meet his gaze, there was no pity reflected in his features. Only compassion and a curious kind of understanding.

"Thank you." She drew a deep, shuddering breath. "I thought I'd passed that stage long ago." Her sad smile caught at his heart. "I guess I owe you an explanation."

His eyes, watchful and concerned, searched her face. "I had to know the truth," he said quietly. "But you don't have to tell me anything you don't want to."

"I know," she whispered. "But I—I think I'd like to."

His gaze never wavered as he lifted her hand and let her knuckles graze his cheek. "Why don't we walk down by the lake?" he suggested. The action was comfortably familiar and lent her the courage that had eluded her thus far.

Tyler laced his fingers through hers, the touch of his hand strong and reassuring around hers. They began to walk, their steps taking them aimlessly along the shore of the lake.

He learned how she had married Rick when she was barely nineteen; how she had forsaken her own dream of finishing college to put Rick through instead.

"My parents had some reservations about us marrying so young, especially when Katie came along so soon. Maybe that's why I was so determined that Rick succeed. I was so proud of him when he graduated and got a job with a computer software firm in Milwaukee. I supported him, I encouraged him. I kept the house and the kids spotless. I . . ." Her voice wavered. "I thought I was the perfect wife."

"Which only made it that much harder when he left?" Their steps came to a halt. His eyes encouraged her.

The still of evening settled around their motionless figures. The world grew hushed and still; for an instant she heard nothing but the sound of her own ragged breathing.

"Yes," she said unevenly. She stared out across the lake, where waning sunbeams blazed a meandering trail of amber and gold, her throat so tight it was a moment before she could resume.

"He called from the airport in Milwaukee one day." Cass squeezed her eyes shut. "God, I'll never forget what he said! At first I was sure he was joking when he told me he wasn't coming home. Then he started talking about how bored and dissatisfied he was . . . how the five of us were like a noose around his neck . . . how he just couldn't take the responsibility anymore. . . . He just wanted to get away and start a whole new life. . . ."

Tyler didn't have to look at her to know how shocked and shattered she had been; he could hear it in her voice, in the way her hand gripped his so tightly that her nails dug into his palm.

"Cass." His voice was scratchy. "Trisha said she didn't know where he was. You never heard from him again . . . at all?"

She shook her head. Her gaze slid away from his. "At first I thought he'd be back. But weeks went by—and then months. I was confused and angry and bitter. Most of all I was scared. We got by with the money in the savings account—Rick took some, but not all of it—but after that I didn't know how the kids and I would get along. I hadn't worked since before Todd was born, so I had no marketable skills. If I hadn't done volunteer work at the school, I'm not sure they'd have hired me."

Listening to her tortured voice, a slow burn began to spread along Tyler's veins. If Rick Lawrence had been there in front of him, he'd have torn him apart with a great deal of pleasure.

"You know what hurt the most?" Cass's voice had grown so low he had to strain to hear. "I remember Sam sobbing in my arms the day I had to tell the kids Rick was never coming back. She kept asking, 'Why? Why did Daddy leave us?'" Her voice was raspy with tears both shed and unshed. "I didn't have an answer for her—I still don't."

"It wasn't your fault, Cass." Tyler's voice was low but fierce. "Surely you know that. It was his inadequacies, not yours, that caused the problem."

Inadequate. Cass winced, for that single word summed up exactly how she'd felt during those miserable days when she'd been so alone.

"I know," she said finally. "But it's easy to forget at times like that."

Somehow they found themselves back where they had started, standing on the deck behind his house. He paused, his eyes roving over her face. Though her expression was still faintly clouded, he was relieved she no longer looked so haunted.

"Are you okay?" he asked quietly.

She nodded.

"Really?"

"Really." Though her smile was a little watery, it appeared to be the genuine article.

"Good," he murmured, never taking his eyes from her face. "Because I'd hate to think I was taking advantage of you." His head dipped closer.

Her breath tumbled to a standstill. The certainty skittered through her that he was going to kiss her. She felt an unreasoning disappointment when he didn't.

"Why would you think that?" She fought a sudden sensation of giddiness.

His thumb, pleasantly rough, skimmed the sloping line of her jaw. "Because tonight you're all mine, lady. And I think a nice long soak in my Jacuzzi is just what the doctor ordered."

Cass sighed. "What is this?" she chided gently. "Tyler to the rescue? You were there the day my hot-water heater caught on fire. You were there for us the next day, just like you've been there all summer." But he wouldn't be there forever, and the thought was like a blow to the heart. Her laugh was shaky. "This is getting to be a habit, wouldn't you say?"

Yes, he thought, staring at her mouth. *And addictive, too.*

He wondered if she was aware of how much he longed to drag her into his arms and lose himself inside her—and how precarious his control really was. He yearned to sweep them both into a world of sweet oblivion, a world that had no past, no haunted memories, a world where only the two of them existed.

But Tyler was just as determined that the next step, whether forward or back, should be up to Cass. Nonetheless, he wasn't averse to prodding her carefully in the right direction.

"I'm harmless," he told her blandly. "Surely you know that by now."

His gaze captured hers. They were so close she could see the tiny network of lines fanning out from his eyes. The tremor of reaction she experienced was only partly due to his nearness. The rest was due to the silent question she could see.

All at once the words he'd spoken earlier echoed in her mind. *You're all mine, lady. It's just the two of us....* Her heart seemed to tremble, then stand still. She thought of Tyler seducing her, then daringly took the thought one step further...making love to her.

Harmless? she echoed belatedly. He was anything *but* harmless, and if she were wise, she'd remember that.

But Cass wasn't feeling very wise just now. She was tired of being sane and sensible, and was suddenly only too willing to be bold and daring...if only for tonight.

She followed when he stepped into the house. "Can I trust you not to lead me astray?" she murmured.

Her teasing caught Tyler off guard, but only for an instant. He closed the door behind her and discovered her eyes were as clear and blue as summer skies.

He tapped his chin thoughtfully and assumed a cautious expression. "Perhaps a better question would be whether I can trust *you* not to lead *me* astray."

She duplicated his smile, her own a little hesitant and tentative. Seeing it roused an odd tightening in Tyler's chest. He felt both possessive and protective of this woman who was usually so fiery and independent. He didn't know what tonight would bring; he didn't care. It was enough just to be with her.

Upstairs in his bedroom, he crossed to the bath. Cass, plagued by a touch of uncertainty and praying it didn't show, trailed behind and stood in the doorway while he stepped up to the tub and reached across. Water began gushing from the faucets.

He straightened, hands on hips, watching as the tub began to fill. Cass paused, taking in the scene before her. Billowing steam fluttered toward the ceiling, where a fan lazily stirred the sultry air. Lush greenery filled every corner. As it had the first time, the room struck her as lush and exotic, sensual and earthy. It made her think of all things wild and wanton.

Her toes curled into the thick pile carpeting. A low-grade panic seized her. She didn't belong here; she was out of her depth. She didn't appreciate the grating little voice inside that reminded her Ms. Sexy Brunette—Suzanne—would have been right at home in such surroundings. The situation wasn't improved when Tyler switched off the overhead light. Her indecision tripled as a circle of lights began to glow above the tub. The room was filled with a soft amber haze.

It was disconcerting to discover Tyler's eyes upon her, dark and depthless, even more so when he tugged her inside.

The door closed behind her with a click.

For a moment there was total silence. Then she heard him murmur, "Well, Cass? Still think my bathroom is decadent?"

"More than ever."

He laughed at her prompt, bluntly spoken response. Tyler didn't mind, however. He was glad to see she was back to normal, direct and alert.

"And I suppose you think I'm depraved as well," he said cheerfully.

"Not just yet," she allowed, then was amazed to feel the beginnings of a smile tug at her lips. "Though I think I'll reserve judgment for a while."

Their eyes met and held for a long, altogether comfortable moment. Then, with an ease clearly born of long familiarity, he pulled his shirt over his head and dropped it onto the floor.

His hands went to his belt buckle.

The next thing she knew, his slacks had shimmied down his legs. Cass was too stunned—perhaps too full of awe—to say anything when she saw that his undershorts were about to go next.

She sucked in a huge mouthful of air and averted her head, but to no avail. The mirrored walls reflected his image from all sides. There was nowhere she could look without confronting Tyler in full male glory.

And he *was* glorious. His body was superbly fashioned. Her gaze lingered helplessly on the cleanly sculpted lines of his back and buttocks as he stretched to pull two thick bath sheets from a shelf. Then he turned, his body outlined in stark, vivid clarity just before he climbed into the tub. Her mind-stealing glimpse of his virility left her in no doubt of his masculine endowments.

Her breath tumbled out in a rush.

Tyler turned his head to regard her through half-closed lids. "Come on in," he invited. "The water's just right."

Until now, she foolishly hadn't given a thought as to what they would wear—or wouldn't—in the Jacuzzi. But Tyler clearly expected her to follow his lead.

His eyes were dark and fathomless, burning like torches in the night. "What's taking you so long?" he murmured.

Cass just shook her head. Speech was impossible. Her tongue was still glued to the roof of her mouth. Her entire being was in chaos.

He sighed. "Cass," he said, and his tone was faintly scolding. "Never let it be said that I don't respect a lady's wishes. You'll note that my hands are on the table—" he smiled ruefully "—or in this case, the water."

His message couldn't have been more implicit. Nothing was going to happen tonight that she didn't want. His assurance seemed to release some of the pent-up tension inside her and lent her the courage she so desperately needed.

Her feet shuffled forward as if of their own volition. Her mouth was bone-dry when she pulled her sweater over her head and added it to the pile of Tyler's clothes. Her slacks came next. All too soon only her bra and panties were left.

Did he watch her as she had watched him? The thought made her shiver. Hands that weren't entirely steady fumbled with the clasp of her bra. She kicked off her panties, then hurriedly lowered herself into the tub, thankful the shadows hid her burning cheeks.

"Feels good, doesn't it?"

His chest brushed her bare shoulder as he stretched his arms along the sides of the tub. Cass was consumed with an awareness that was near painful in intensity. She nodded and huddled deeper into the water.

For several moments the only sound was that of quietly bubbling water. She closed her eyes, and still she could see the shape of him—long, naked limbs, broad chest matted in golden fur, steely muscles sheathed in skin of heavy satin. He shifted and Cass suppressed an inward tremor. The length of his thigh rode gently against hers for half a heartbeat. Their closeness was suddenly unbearably intimate.

Tyler watched the muted light turn her hair to spun gold. His glance slid down her neck to gleaming, slender shoulders. Her hair was coiled into a loose knot on her crown. Damp tendrils clung to her nape and forehead. With her hair up, her head down, she looked incredibly childlike.

"You're pretty," he said suddenly.

Her head shot up at his unexpected praise. Her face stung with warmth, but it was the warmth of pleasure. Did he have any idea what his whispered confession, the dark velvet of his voice, did to her? It played on her senses like the elusive brush of a feather. She could almost feel his lips on hers, firm and warm and persuasive.

She stared at a particularly fascinating spot in the opposite wall. "Tyler," she murmured, "you don't have to say that."

Tyler felt his heart turn over. To him she had never looked more beautiful or more vulnerable. Lord knows, she had no reason to be ashamed. The bare skin of her shoulders gleamed a honey gold, offering tantalizing glimpses of the treasures that lay below. Just thinking about her full breasts, crowned by dusky-pink nipples, tested his control to the limit. She was all he had hoped for . . . all he ever wanted.

His eyes captured hers. "I said it because I wanted to. Don't you know that?"

Her laugh was as shaky as she felt inside. "Well, you obviously weren't looking or you'd have noticed a stretch mark or two. . . ."

"But I was," he confirmed. There was another heartbeat of silence. "You're pretty," he said again. "Everywhere."

His voice had dropped to a whisper. The husky cadence of his tone made it almost a caress. He touched her nowhere, yet she could feel the promise of his touch in every cell of her body.

She looked away in confusion. The words were all that she longed to hear . . . and all she feared. The woman in her reveled in his praise, but she was unaccustomed to such attention and not quite sure how to handle it.

"Would you rub my shoulders?"

Her eyes flew to his in startled surprise. "What?"

"Rub my shoulders." He presented his back to her, then glanced over his shoulder. "Please."

Cass hesitated. His skin looked like oiled teak. Her fingers tingled at the mere thought of touching his firm, taut flesh. Slowly, reluctantly, she placed her hands upon his shoulders. At first awkwardly, then more firmly, she began to knead his muscles.

After a few seconds he sighed. "Lord, that feels good," he muttered. "Anyone ever tell you you have the magic touch?"

She didn't bother to answer, compressing her lips when she discovered a particularly hard knot near one shoulder blade. "You're like a board," she said, only half kidding. "What on earth did you do to get like this? I thought you were celebrating today."

"I spent most of the day hunched over my computer to get the newsletter finished, so we could celebrate *tonight*."

"Serves you right then," she said, wrinkling her nose. Her hands continued to stroke and knead, rhythmically easing the tightness from his shoulders.

Tyler closed his eyes and relaxed. It wasn't long before he realized her touch was having a profound effect on his body. The feel of her palms sliding over his wet skin drove him wild. Her breath fluttered over his cheek when she leaned forward to apply more pressure. He felt the peaks of her breasts brush against his back and went a little crazy, imagining how they would feel in his hands.

"Cass," he gasped when he could stand it no longer. "This is torture." He slid around to face her.

"It still hurts?" Her voice was breathless, but she couldn't help it. The warmth of his skin seemed to permeate her very soul. Water glistened like tiny diamonds in the rough fur on his chest. She fought a nearly irresistible urge to slide her palms over the dense gold down. "Where?" she asked.

He dragged her fingertips to his lips. "Here." His hand over hers, he guided it down and opened her fingers against his heart.

She looked up and caught the hungry look on his face. There was no trace of laughter as his eyes bored into hers. Only longing, a longing so intense she felt everything inside her grow weak.

There was a riot of emotions churning away inside her. What was he trying to say? she wondered frantically. She wasn't sure she dared speculate. Her experience with Rick had taught her to take nothing for granted. *Please,* she begged silently. *Don't toy with me.*

Her gaze was the first to slip away. She lowered her eyes slowly, then gasped as she realized the path they had taken. A quickening heat stormed through her as she confronted the bold and irrefutable evidence of male desire.

Tyler smiled crookedly. "The magic touch again?"

Cass swallowed and tore her eyes from the sight.

He felt his smile fade, his face grow taut, his expression almost grim. "Cass." He spoke her name with quiet deliberation when he saw that he had her attention. "Maybe this wasn't such a good idea, after all. Because I'm afraid I can't be around you like this without wanting to hold you, to touch you... to kiss you." He paused, aware the slightly ragged edge in his voice was revealing the tight rein he'd placed on himself.

"I won't be angry if you decide you want to leave. But if you do, it has to be now, Cass. Because if you stay—" his voice reached an even lower pitch "—I can't promise I won't make love to you."

The air was suddenly filled with a brittle tension. She felt his gaze on her face, questioning but unerringly direct. Inside her brain a warning bell went off. Her mind was filled with unwanted, uninvited thoughts and forbidden yearnings.

Tyler, she thought helplessly, hopelessly. Was this right or wrong? She wasn't sure. She knew only that after tonight there would be no turning back.

But at least he was being honest with her. How could she be less than honest with him?

He made her forget all the reasons why this was all wrong, all the reasons why this shouldn't be happening. He made her forget everything but her need for him.

She couldn't fight it any longer. She couldn't fight him . . . or herself.

A hand tentatively touched his chest. The other crept up to join it. Her eyes shyly sought his.

"I—I don't want to leave," she confessed, unable to disguise the tremor in her voice. Suddenly it was all gushing out and there wasn't a thing she could do to stop it, nor did she want to. "I want to stay. Tonight. Here with you. I want you, too. . . . Tyler, I want you so much. . . ."

12

THE WORDS LINGERED in the air like the plumes of steam rising from the frothing water.

Tyler pulled back and searched her face. He saw no shadows, no doubt, only a tremulous yearning that met and matched his own.

His need for her was so intense it bordered on pain. He wanted her so much he felt like a spring about to unwind, but inside he was shaking.

Just when Cass could stand the waiting and the tension no longer, his hands came down upon her shoulders. She could look no higher than the wild tangle of hairs that filled the hollow of his throat.

"God, I hope you mean that," he said in a voice that caused her to tremble all over again. "Because, lady, I think our time just ran out." His eyes darkened. "Come here," he whispered.

The rough thread of need in his voice thrilled her. Her arms slipped around his neck, freely and without any urging from him. But just as their lips would have met, he raised his head. "I think I'd better settle this while I'm still thinking straight. I know you didn't plan on this tonight," he said huskily. His eyes were gently probing. "Do I need to use—?"

Cass understood immediately. Her gaze focused shyly on the hollow of his throat. "It's okay," she whispered. "I had my tubes tied after Trisha was born."

Tyler pressed her head into his shoulder. "There won't be any interruptions this time." His eyes shone fiercely as he raised his head and stared into her face. "You know that, don't you?"

The words were both a warning and a plea. She knew what he was doing. He wanted to make sure that she was absolutely certain this was what she wanted. He could have taken what she offered without question; the fact that he cared enough to give her one last chance to change her mind touched her deeply.

Her fingers stole to his cheek. "Now that sounds like a reason to celebrate," she teased with a quavering little smile.

It was all he needed to hear. And it would have to be enough, Tyler thought vaguely, for his control had just run out. His gaze roved over her face, seeking to commit each feature to memory. Desire made her eyes breathtakingly brilliant. Her lips were parted. Waiting. Wanting.

His arms tightened. It was all he could do to keep from crushing her against him. Instead he hauled her onto his lap, lowered his head and kissed her until their hearts were pressed together and his mind was spinning. Yet all the while he fed on her sweetly giving mouth, exploring all the wild, wonderful ways he'd wanted to kiss her during those long, lonely nights without her.

She gave a tiny jolt of pleasure when his tongue touched hers. He stroked with a delicate demand, loving the way her tongue initiated a daringly intricate skirmish with his that left both of them gasping.

He dragged his mouth away, feeling as if he were drowning. But there was no respite from the storm of desire that consumed him. The buoyancy of the water revealed the naked bounty of her breasts. The trembling thrust of pink, swollen tips bobbing against his chest tormented him like a feast before a man starved for months. The sight filled him with a surge of longing that was purely primitive, purely male.

He rested his forehead against hers. "Oh, Cass." There was an odd catch in his voice. "This is driving me crazy. Touching you . . . yet not touching you. I have to feel you. I have to touch you. Not just part of you, but all of you . . . all of you."

The words sent stark, vivid images tumbling through her brain. But she didn't grasp his meaning until his arm slid under her knees. With a surge of power he was rising, stepping out of the water.

She clutched at his shoulders. "Hey!" she protested with a breathless laugh. "You're about to shatter the myth. How can I think of this room as decadent if we leave so soon?"

His laugh was as breathless as hers. "I'll make it up to you." In the bedroom he lowered her to the floor next to the bed, grabbed a towel and began to dry her, hurriedly and not very well. Then he reached for her. His arms closed around her and pulled her tight and close; his mouth sought hers. Reacting instinctively, her arms circled his neck. She went up on tiptoe and pressed against him so they were welded together from head to toe.

Tyler thought he'd died and gone to heaven. His mouth opened wider over hers.

A sweet, awful yearning began to build inside her. He kissed her over and over, endless, drugging kisses that lasted forever and ended much too soon. She was achingly aware of the turgid force of his desire straining against the hollow of her stomach. His hands came down and closed around her buttocks. The movement almost convulsive, he lifted and cupped her hard and tight against him, fusing their hips. Her senses ran wild. She had no idea where her body ended and his began.

She was only vaguely aware when he pulled her down and onto the bed beside him. Her entire body was attuned only to his, the brush of his hands on her skin, his fingertips faintly rough, but incredibly arousing.

"You're so pretty," he whispered hoarsely. He was held spellbound by the trembling thrust of her breasts, her skin all honey and gold in the muted lamplight.

Her gaze followed his. Her mouth grew dry at the sight of his dark hands splayed against her ribs. Those same hands slid relentlessly upward, his thumbs tracing lingering circles over the burgeoning fullness of her breasts, inching ever closer to their dark, straining centers. Her nipples grew tight and pebble hard. Her nerves were stretched to a screaming pitch, and she waited impatiently. Yet knowing they both watched and savored her body's response only heightened the anticipation.

She shivered when his thumbs skimmed her nipples, tantalizing and tormenting, but that was only the beginning. He shifted slightly; his head began to move lower. She swallowed a breathless little cry as he claimed one tender summit with his lips. His tongue was an instrument both of torture and delight as he bathed the quivering bud with moist heat, then initiated a slow, mind-spinning tugging that reached clear to her heart.

Her breathing was rapid and shallow when at last his head came up. Her eyes flickered open under heavy lids. Tyler's arms slid around her and he eased to his side, taking her with him. His hand wasn't entirely steady as he smoothed a tendril of hair from her cheek.

"Oh, Cass." Her name was both a prayer and a plea. "Do you have any idea how it's been for me these last few weeks? I've spent practically every waking moment thinking about you.... At night I've dreamed about you...dreamed I was kissing you...holding you...wanting you so much I thought I'd die."

Cass caught her breath. His husky declaration disarmed her. Captivated her. Her pulse began to clamor as his eyes swept over her, dark and searing. Tyler looked at her like a man looks at a desirable woman. Had Rick ever looked at her like this? she wondered dizzily. She didn't know. Right now she didn't care.

Tyler made her feel as if she were the most beautiful woman on earth. As if she was very special and oh, so cherished. He looked at her...like a lover.

Her heart turned over. Something inside seemed to blossom and grow. Cass couldn't ever remember needing anyone the way she needed Tyler right now.

"Oh, Tyler," she whispered achingly. "That's the way it's been for me, too."

He pressed a kiss to the hand she stretched out. His laugh was husky. "Good, because I've been going crazy wondering how it would feel to have you touch me. Here." He brought her fingers to his chest. "And here." His hand over hers, he flattened her palm and guided it down his flat stomach. Through a fiery haze of pleasure she felt her fingertips glide lightly over warm, hair-matted skin.

His gaze captured hers. "And here." The pitch of his voice fell lower still, his hand completing its plundering journey downward.

Her breathing tumbled to a standstill. In the fraction of a second allotted her, she realized he wanted her to touch him in bold, intimate ways. Nor could she deny the overwhelming need to do exactly that.

Helpless, her fingers curled around his hardness. Her first tentative touch sent a jolt of pleasure crashing through both of them. His eyes closed, his breathing grew harsh and rasping, the muscles of his stomach clenched as she discovered the most boldly aggressive part of him. Watching him, knowing her touch pleased him, made her want to weep with joy.

When he could bear the delicious torment no longer, he groaned and rolled her onto her back and sealed her lips with his. She could taste the hunger in his mouth; her own was just as fierce. She felt surrounded, immersed in the sight and scent and feel of this man.

His fingers slid through the dark fur guarding her most vulnerable spot, seeking and finding the tiny bud, hidden deep within dewy folds of velvet flesh. His fingertips began a slow, tortuous motion that rendered her nearly mindless. She moaned, a ragged, husky sound that sounded alien to her ears.

"Tyler..." Her hands dug into the sleek flesh of his shoulders.

He caught the strangled sound in the back of his throat. "I want you," he said into her mouth, and then again. "I want you so much. I want to fill you, feel you tight and warm around me...your legs wrapped around mine...."

Joy and pleasure spun through her at the sharp need she heard in his voice. Strong hands slid beneath her buttocks; he lowered himself slowly against the intimate cradle of her thighs. She gasped as the potent strength of his manhood parted tender petals of warmth. Then he was with her, inside her, stealing her breath and scattering her senses.

His moan mingled with hers. For a heart-stopping moment he lay completely still, clasped within the heated velvet of her body. His eyes closed against a pleasure so exquisite it was almost unbearable.

Time stood still as their bodies began the sensuous rhythm of love, slow and deep. They were lost in a passion-drenched world where only the two of them existed. Hands caressed, lips blended and merged, until neither could stand the sweetly restrained pace of their loving.

"Tyler! Oh, Tyler!" Her hands slid into the golden roughness of his hair. She clasped him to her, fusing their mouths. Her legs rose and tightened around his hips, as if she sought to capture and hold him forever.

Tyler was lost. The feel of her legs hugging him stripped away the last vestiges of control. He plunged harder. Deeper. Faster and faster. This was just the way he'd dreamed it, only reality was so much better. The tempo of his thrusts reached a soul-shattering intensity that sent them spinning toward the edge.

Together they reached that shimmering peak of pleasure. Knowing he shared her release, she experienced a feeling of unity, of oneness and completion, unlike anything she'd ever felt before. And in that moment, heart and mind in tandem, Cass suddenly knew....

She loved him. God help her, she loved him.

A WARM, BUTTERFLY KISS floated across her lips. Cass stirred. The kiss came again, tantalizing and elusive and beckoning. Her mind still snarled in the mists of slumber, she felt herself smile and drowsily give herself up to the wondrous melding of their lips.

"If you keep on tempting me," said a laughter-filled voice against her cheek, "you may never get that breakfast in bed you've always wanted."

She frowned and blinked sleepily. While she wondered a little at his self-satisfied expression, he nodded at the nightstand beside her. Her eyes widened when she saw a fully laden tray, complete with French toast, bacon, and a tiny vase filled with violets.

Her gaze shot up to his. "You fixed breakfast for me?" Her expression reflected both wonder and pleasure.

Tyler chuckled, pleased at her reaction. "Aren't you the woman who told the boys in her cooking class that breakfast in bed would be heaven? I, for one," he went on lightly, "was a captive audience." His own definition of heaven was a little different, having nothing to do with food and everything to do with the woman who had slept in his arms last night...when they had let each other sleep, of course.

He reached for the tray. Cass sat up and tugged the sheet over her bare breasts. But once he slid the tray onto her lap, she discovered that balancing the tray, wielding her fork and keeping her breasts covered posed a problem. Tyler's weight beside her on the mattress threatened to rip the sheet from her grasp any second.

She glanced almost accusingly at the dark blue robe he wore. "No need to be modest," he told her and chuckled. "You weren't last night."

Her heart began to clamor. Her predicament with the tray was forgotten. She could feel once more the imprint of his body on hers, the warm, welcoming way her body had closed around his heated fullness.

All at once she could look no higher than the hollow of his throat. No, she thought vaguely. Modest was the one thing she hadn't been last night. She had been eager and avid to discover all she could about Tyler, as eager as he had been for her. The realization was both exhilarating and unsettling.

There was a rumble of soft laughter deep in his chest. "I could feed you," he offered.

"I wouldn't have a problem," she said dryly, "if you would get me a shirt or something to wear."

His gaze lingeringly traced the enticing outline of her body beneath the sheet. "That would be criminal, considering how long I've waited to see you like this."

"You saw all there is to see last night!"

He ran a fingertip along her collarbone. "I did," he stated brashly, "and I find I'm very anxious to repeat the experience."

Her pulse skittered alarmingly. "Tyler." His name was spoken on a half laugh, half groan. "You're impossible."

No, he thought suddenly. He was in love....

With a sigh, he moved to the other side of the bed. Propping his elbow up on the mattress, he stretched out on his side next to her. He found being with Cass like this, teasing and laughing after a long night of making love, altogether natural. It filled him with a feeling of contentment unlike anything he had ever experienced before.

And he didn't have to wonder why; he knew.

He watched her take her first bite of French toast. "Well," he prompted, "how is it? And before you answer, I'll have you know I've spent nearly every morning the last month, trying to make perfect French toast and pancakes—and all to please you. In fact, I doubt I'll ever eat either again."

He loved her impish smile, the way her eyes filled with a hundred sparkling lights. "It's perfect," she pronounced. "And having breakfast in bed is just what I thought it would be—" she sighed "—it's heavenly." Her smile made his heart turn over. "Thank you, Tyler."

His gaze slipped to her mouth. "Why, thank you, kind lady. I have no objection to indulging you again." With one fingertip he reached over and blotted a drop of syrup from the corner of her lip. Holding her gaze, he sucked his finger clean.

Cass felt her heart constrict. The look in his eyes was warm and inviting, fraught with unspoken messages. Yet Cass wasn't sure she dared interpret his meaning. A frisson of panic touched her spine. What would happen next? Last night had meant the world to her. But what had it meant to Tyler? He had made no promises. No guarantees. He certainly hadn't said he loved her....
There was a wrenching pain in the region of her heart.

Face it, lady, chided a tiny little voice in the back of her mind. *You can't plan on waking up to Tyler every*

*day for the rest of your life, so you might as well accept
it right now.*

The sooner, the better.

The French toast that had tasted so delicious a moment earlier suddenly tasted like ashes. Cass finally set the tray aside. But as she turned back, the warm weight of Tyler's hand settled upon her stomach.

"What should we do today?" The merest hint of laughter lurked in his tone. His crooked smile was disarming. "We could stay in bed all day and just laze around... or stay in bed all day and *fool* around...."

A pang knifed through her. *Don't do this to me,* the voice inside cried. *I want more than just your body. I want more than just a day. More than just a night.* But fear kept the words buried deep in her heart, the fear that perhaps that was all *he* wanted.

His fingers initiated a slow, rousing stroke that robbed her of breath. She steeled herself against the quiver of desire that shot through her.

She shook her head, somehow managing a semblance of a smile. "I really should be going home."

He frowned.

She drew up her legs toward her chest, unable to look at him. "I have a million things to do and—"

"And the kids won't be home until tomorrow. Why don't we take advantage and take this time for us?"

"I can't," she said unevenly.

Tyler sat up slowly. "Why, Cass? Tell me why."

The back of his knuckles grazed her cheek. But it was the gentleness in his voice that was almost her undoing. "You know why," she whispered.

Tyler did, but right now he wished like hell that he didn't. "Because of last night."

"Yes." She couldn't hide her misery.

His gaze was riveted to her profile. "Maybe you'd like to explain that."

Her fingers clenched and unclenched on the sheet. "Tyler, I . . . I can't play at love like this. . . ."

"Play?" He swore hotly. Hands on her shoulders, he pulled her around to face him. "Dammit, Cass, is that what you think we're doing? I wanted last night to happen, do you hear? I've wanted it for a long time."

She spoke unthinkingly, saying the first thing that popped into her head. "But if it happened once, it could happen again!"

His hands fell from her shoulders. "You regret it!" he said incredulously. His expression changed radically. Another time, another place, and Cass might have found it amusing. Now the hurt that flitted across his features only made her want to cry.

"You don't understand!" she cried wildly, stopping short of calling last night a mistake. How could she call the most wonderful night of her life a mistake?

"Maybe we just got carried away." Her voice was very low. "Maybe we were just fooling ourselves. . . ."

"And maybe it shouldn't happen again." He glared at her. "That's what you think, isn't it?"

"What do you expect me to say, Tyler?" She was almost grateful for the surge of anger that washed through her veins. "Are we supposed to pop in and out for a quickie whenever the urge strikes one of us? That should give the neighbors plenty to talk about." Her

tone was mutinous. "I won't have my children exposed
to that kind of gossip. Surely you can understand that."

"Damned right I do," he snapped. "But there
wouldn't be a problem if we were married."

13

HER JAW SAGGED. Her eyes locked with Tyler's. In the shocked silence that followed she had the strangest sensation that Tyler was as taken aback by his pronouncement as she.

An unseen hand seemed to close around her heart and squeeze. She was suddenly shaking, grappling for emotions gone suddenly haywire, struggling for control.

She slid from the bed. Her movements jerky, she gathered up her clothes and began to dress. *Married...If we were married...* The phrase kept running through her brain. She shook her head as if to clear it.

Exactly where the thought had come from, Tyler didn't know. But now that the initial shock had passed, he wasn't at all appalled by the idea of marrying Cass. Far from it.

A smile dallied at his lips. He watched her rise from the bed. Though he was rather puzzled by her reaction, it didn't dim his swell of satisfaction.

"Cass."

"What?" She thrust her arms through the sleeves of her sweater.

"Didn't you hear me?"

Her head popped through the neck. Darn him, anyway! Why was he wearing that smug half smile? "I heard you," she muttered. "And I'll have you know, if this is your idea of a joke, I don't find it at all funny!"

Tyler's smile withered. "I wasn't joking," he stated flatly.

"No?" Even to her own ears, her tone bordered on the hysterical. "I recall you telling me, and not so long ago, that you've never seriously considered marriage."

He thrust a hand through his hair. "I hadn't," he admitted. There was a long-drawn-out pause. "Until now."

"Really!" The word was fairly flung at him.

"Really."

"And now you've decided you want to marry me? My God, Tyler, how much thought have you even given the idea?"

"All that I need to," he said, but not before a twinge of guilt crossed his features.

Cass might have laughed if she hadn't been crying inside. "Tyler," she said raggedly. "You can't make a snap decision like this when it comes to something like marriage...."

"I want you," he said softly, deliberately. "I love you. Isn't that enough?" The intensity of his tone captured her attention in a flash.

She could have wept at the tenderness she saw on his face. He loved her. *He loved her.* But all at once she was raw and bleeding inside.

"I want it to be enough," she whispered. "God, I wish it were!"

Tyler stared at her. There was a funny, awful feeling flitting around inside him. When he finally spoke, his tone was very quiet. "Why do I have the feeling you're throwing up hurdles that don't exist?"

"Hurdles that don't exist!" It was a cry of outrage, a cry of pain. "Tyler, you're forgetting I have four children who go where I go. Are you saying you have no qualms about taking on not only a wife but a ready-made family, as well?"

The question hung between them, creating a brittle tension that was unbearable for both of them. Watching him—watching the doubt and guilt chase across his face, Cass died a little inside.

Finally he emitted a long, weary sigh. "What can I say, Cass? I won't lie and say it doesn't scare me, because it does. You were right when you said I've never given much thought to marriage, and I've given even less to the idea of having children. But your kids like me. I like them."

He took a deep breath, praying he wasn't handling this all wrong, yet very much afraid that he was. "I know you're scared, too. But what matters is that you and I have something very special." He paused for the space of a heartbeat. "I believe in *us*, Cass. Why can't you?"

He stretched out a hand. All at once Cass jerked away, wincing at the hurt that flashed across his strong features. But she felt that if he touched her, she'd break apart.

She stared at him helplessly. "What if it's not enough? What if we find out too late that we're all wrong for each other? What then, Tyler? The damage would be done. It's not just me I'm thinking of, either. You're like a hero to the kids! How do you think they'd feel if you walked out on them the way their father did?"

His eyes narrowed. "You're pushing me away, Cass. Dammit, you know you are! And why are you so damned certain that's what's going to happen?"

"How can you be so certain it *won't*? Rick didn't want us. He didn't want me. He didn't want the kids! How long before you decide you don't want us, too?"

The pain in her voice brought agony to his heart. But Tyler was deeply, bitterly frustrated and in no less pain than Cass. His mouth twisted. "You think I'm like Rick," he accused.

"Maybe you are," she cried wildly. "It was a snap decision when you quit your job in Chicago. You told me yourself! And moving here wasn't much more than a whim, either! And now you've decided you want to marry me—" she snapped her fingers "—just like that! Can you blame me for doubting you? My God, the last thing I need in my life is another man like Rick!"

Every muscle in Tyler's body went rigid. "Thank you very much," he said, his lips barely moving. "At least I know now what you think of me."

Their eyes locked. His face grew clear of all expression, but in the fraction of a second allotted her, her mind recorded a fleeting impression of fury. She'd never seen Tyler so angry, she realized vaguely. She'd never seen him angry, period! Only then did she know she had wounded him.

But the knowledge didn't lessen her own torment. If anything, her confusion deepened.

She stumbled numbly to the bed. "Oh, Tyler." Her breath came jerkily. "Tyler, I'm sorry. I didn't mean for it to come out like that." She pressed trembling fingers against her forehead.

Suddenly she was babbling, knowing she wasn't making any sense, but unable to stop. "I didn't expect this from you, Tyler. And I don't know what I want anymore. I have to do what's right for me and the kids, but I—I just don't know what it is! I need some time to think this through, but I—I just can't think with you around...."

His face tightened. "Fine," he muttered. "You want me out of the picture, I'll be happy to oblige."

Her head shot up. Stunned, she watched him stalk across the room. She winced when he nearly yanked the closet door off its hinges. "What are you doing?" Her voice was as faint as her heartbeat.

A suitcase thumped heavily to the floor. "I'm packing."

Nervously, she rose to her feet. "You're leaving?"

"Obviously."

"Where are you going?" To her everlasting shame, hot tears pricked the back of her throat.

"Chicago. I'll stay at my parents' condo." His expression, like his voice, was icy and distant. "While I'm there I'll probably renew some business contacts. I'd planned to handle it by phone, but I might as well do it in person."

She watched him dump an armload of shirts across the bed. "I didn't know you were planning this—"

"I wasn't."

Her heart toppled to the floor. "But you're going anyway? Just like that?"

He gave her a long, cool look. "Yes."

A tight knot of dread began to coil in her stomach. She struggled to force her voice past the aching constriction in her throat. "When will you be back?" She didn't dare ask *if* he would be back.

He straightened, his posture rigidly dignified. His hesitation was all that she'd feared. "I don't know," he said finally. "A few days. Maybe a week."

Maybe never....

Her retreat was awkward and halting, their goodbyes came out stilted and so polite she wanted to scream. It wasn't until she was back in her own house that she became aware she hadn't even told him she loved him.

Would it have made any difference? Would Tyler have stayed if she had uttered those three little words—words that held all the hope and fear that filled her soul? She didn't know.

Now she never would.

HE LEFT AN HOUR LATER. Cass stood at the living-room window. She stared outside with dry eyes and hungry heart. Was this the last time she would ever see him? She tried to dismiss the idea as paranoid and ridiculous. After all, he'd given her no reason to think he wouldn't be back.

The kids were crushed when they found out Tyler had gone. Stifling a twinge of guilt, Cass explained he'd had to return to Chicago unexpectedly on business. Katie eyed her rather oddly. Or did she only imagine it? But Samantha was the one who pointed out what Cass had overlooked until then.

She scooted up close to her mother, her voice very small. "Where's Missy?"

Cass balked. "I'm not sure, honey. I guess Tyler must have taken her along."

Samantha looked stricken. Cass tried to stop her when she tore out the back door. When the little girl returned a few minutes later, she seemed utterly heartbroken.

"Missy's leash is gone. Tyler always leaves it hanging by the back door so I can get it whenever I want to walk her." Tears stood in her eyes. "He could have left Missy with us, Mom. Why didn't he? Did I do something wrong? Did he leave and take Missy because he's mad at me?"

Cass flinched at the wounded look in her daughter's eyes. For a horrifying instant, it was as if the two of them had been plunged back in time. Sam was anxious and fearful, while she felt lost and abandoned and was trying desperately not to show it. She tried to convince herself the situation with Tyler was entirely different from the way things had been with Rick. But the parallels were too obvious for her to ignore.

She hugged her daughter fiercely, even as her mind groped for an answer. "Of course Tyler isn't mad at you, sweetheart. I told you, he had to leave for a few days on business. And remember, you weren't here when he left. Maybe he felt he shouldn't leave Missy without asking you first if you would take care of her."

But while Sam appeared mollified, Cass most definitely was not. Why hadn't Tyler left Missy with them? She could think of only one reason.

Maybe he wasn't coming back, after all.

The next week was far from easy. First thing the next morning Brian, Todd and even David got into a riproaring argument. Even Sara and Samantha bickered. Trisha was irritable because she'd somehow managed to traipse through a patch of poison ivy over the weekend. To top it off, sweet, bubbly Emily was teething and unusually crabby.

But while Cass had plenty to keep her mind occupied throughout the days, the evenings were another story. Samantha and Trish sat on the porch, gazing mournfully at Tyler's house. Todd rode his bike in circles in front of Tyler's driveway, until she got dizzy watching him. She caught Katie peering pensively out the window more than once.

They missed Tyler. And so did their mother—she missed him terribly. She hadn't realized how much a part of their life he'd become . . . until he was no longer a part of it.

She lay in bed one night, piecing together all the reasons why a marriage between them would never work. Yet all she could think of was how she missed the feeling of kinship, of togetherness and belonging, that they had shared. Cass wanted desperately to believe in it. But trust no longer came easily. And trust carried risks she wasn't sure she dared take.

Was she too overprotective of her children? Perhaps. But they needed a stable home life. They needed love. *She* needed love.

She could lie to herself no longer.

She wanted everything she'd once had, everything she'd thought would be hers forever. A home. A husband who loved her as much as she loved him. And she wanted all that she had now, as well. Her independence, her self-esteem, her pride, stubborn though it was.

Tyler had accused her of pushing him away. He'd said he knew how afraid she was. He was right, she acknowledged sadly. She wasn't just scared—she was terrified! Where Tyler was concerned, she felt fear as she'd never felt it before.

She loved him too much to lose him. It was as simple—as complicated—as that.

Her heart twisted. If only he hadn't said he loved her... But he had. *He loved her.* And—miracle of miracles—he wanted to marry her!

The thought sent her spinning into the seventh heaven and beyond. But even as she wanted to hug and pinch herself so she knew she wasn't dreaming, dark despair dragged her rudely back to earth. How could she risk the chance that Tyler might walk away from them as Rick had... and when? Next year? The year after?

On and on the battle raged. A scalding tear seeped from the corner of her eye onto the pillowcase. Then another and another. All too soon the tears became a torrent. She cried for the confusion she felt in Tyler's arms. She cried because she wanted desperately to feel those arms around her now, this very moment....

A hand touched her shoulder. Cass rolled over with a gasp to find Trisha at her bedside. "Mommy?"

She swiped at her cheeks with the back of her hand and sat up. "What, sweetie?"

"Your voice sounds funny. Like Sam's when she's crying." She peered at her anxiously. "Are you crying, Mommy?"

"I'm okay, honey." Cass passed off the little white lie with a tremulous smile and patted the side of the bed. "What about you, though? Why aren't you asleep?"

Trisha climbed up beside her. "My legs itch. I know you told me not to scratch, but I can't help it. Especially right here." She pulled up the hem of her night-gown and exposed her ankle.

Cass switched on the bedside lamp. "Uh-oh," she murmured. "There's a little spot where you've made it bleed."

"It hurts," Trisha said mournfully.

"We'll put a bandage on it and it'll feel better."

Five minutes later Trisha preceded her into the bed-room again, her bandage in place. Cass climbed into bed and pulled Trisha in beside her.

"Mommy?" came a tiny little voice a few seconds later.

Her arms tightened around Trisha's small body. "What, sweetheart?"

"It still hurts."

Cass's thoughts sped straight to Tyler. Her heart twisted painfully. "I know," she whispered.

IF CASS WAS CONFUSED, Tyler was more certain than ever that he wouldn't change his mind. He'd gone off half-cocked when Cass had said she couldn't think with him around; he was both angry and hurt. His split-second decision to head back to Chicago had been more of a reflex action than a conscious choice. But Tyler was well aware he'd thrown her a curve when he an-nounced his intention to leave. Maybe he'd secretly hoped to shock her into seeing what was clear as glass in his own mind.

He knew her too well by now not to sense what was probably going through that pretty head of hers. She was convinced that once he was back in Chicago, he would wholeheartedly embrace all that he'd left behind; that he'd realize what he was missing and decide to stay for good.

And indeed, he was every bit as restless and empty and dissatisfied as he'd been when he left several months ago. But this time there was a far different reason.

He'd been chafing for days already, aching to get back to Cass, yet just as determined to give her the time she'd said she needed. It hadn't been until later, when he'd been thinking more clearly, that he'd begun to fully understand.... In a way, she'd also been asking him to make certain he was sure about his feelings.

So he'd set about doing exactly that. He'd gone out with friends, had lunch with an old group of traders. But nothing had been the same.

It was then that he'd realized . . . he was the one who had changed.

When he'd left Chicago, all he'd really known was that he needed a change. A different career. A different home. He hadn't really intended to change the entire focus of his life, just alter the course somewhat.

He'd never dreamed he'd find someone to fill the hollow place inside him. But somehow Cass and her children had crept into his heart. And now the five of them *were* his life.

From his vantage point thirty stories above Lake Michigan, Tyler stared bleakly at the wind-tossed, murky waves, conscious of a gnawing ache in his gut. Knowing that Cass thought he was like Rick still made him madder than hell. Yet he understood why she was so afraid to believe he could ever be a permanent fixture in her life.

That was the hell of it.

A sound caught his attention. He looked down to find Missy at his feet, gazing up at him with soulful brown eyes.

It seemed Missy didn't like being uprooted any more than he did. There was nowhere for her to run here except in the park, but she was frightened by all the people.

Smiling, he eased down onto one knee. "You don't like it here, do you, girl?"

Missy's tail thumped once as if in agreement.

He ran his hand the length of her body. "I'll bet you miss Sam taking you for a walk every night and playing with the Frisbee."

The dog's ears pricked forward as if she understood every word. His laugh sounded foreign and rusty, even to his own ears.

His smile withered. His hand grew still. An image of Samantha's face flickered into his mind. His heart melted as he remembered how she'd gazed up at her mother when she discovered he owned a dog, her arm around Missy, her eyes bright and shining.

All at once it was as if they all stood there before him, tantalizingly close but just out of reach. He saw Todd with his silly, crooked grin, his features full of mischief; and Trisha, so childlike and forthright and honest, bright blue eyes sparkling impishly. He thought of the four of them beaming while he ate every last crumb of that wonderful, mind-boggling, green birthday cake.

And then there was Cass. How he missed her! His eyes squeezed shut and still he could see her, her honey-gold hair bobbing gently against her neck; he could hear her laugh, that free, carefree laughter he'd heard all too seldom. And he could feel the sweet, supple length of her body beneath his, the sinuous twist of her hips as she took him to heaven.

A heavy tightness gripped his chest. He was overwhelmed by a bone-deep sense of isolation. The air around him grew still and silent. Deep inside, a nagging emptiness rose stark and lonely....

Like a house with all the children gone.

His eyes opened. Missy's head, still gazing at him mournfully, swam into focus.

He scratched the fur behind her ear. "Missy," he said softly, "I think it's time we went home."

14

"TYLER'S BACK!" On Sunday afternoon Samantha banged into the living room, grinning from ear to ear.

Katie laughed and turned fixed, knowing eyes upon her mother. Trisha screamed and leaped to her feet. Todd whooped and charged from the room. Cass half expected to hear bells ring and whistles shrill.

But all she could hear was the pounding of her heart. All at once her blood was singing. *Tyler's back. He's back!*

And suddenly there he was, coming up the walk, surrounded by three of her four children. Her hasty retreat into the kitchen was fueled by a sudden attack of the jitters. Needing to do something—anything—she grabbed the dish towel and began drying dishes.

In the other room she heard Katie's greeting and a deep male voice—Tyler's. There was laughter and excited chatter and more laughter. The front screen slammed several times in rapid succession. The sudden silence was deafening. In the midst of reaching to open the cupboard door, she froze. Her heart plunged to the floor. Had he left so soon? Without seeing her?

"Hello, there," said a voice behind her.

She whirled around and came face-to-face with him. He looked impossibly handsome in wheat-colored slacks and white knit shirt, his eyes as clear and warm as whiskey. His crooked little smile made her heart knock wildly.

She clutched the dish towel as if it were a lifeline. She wanted desperately to say something, but couldn't. It was Tyler who explained the unexpected quiet. "The kids went over to my place to see Missy. And to see what I brought back for them."

"You brought something back for them? That was...sweet of you." Her smile was as faint as her voice, she knew. "They missed you, all of them."

Tyler scrutinized her intently. Her hair was loose and skimmed her shoulders, just the way he liked it. She had on the same pink T-shirt and shorts she'd worn the day they met. Slim, bare feet accented her youthful air.

All at once his heart was thudding painfully. "What about you, Cass? Did you miss me?"

Cass didn't miss his guarded tone. She stared at him, her stomach twisted with hope and fear and a dozen other emotions.

"I didn't know when you'd be back," she blurted. "In fact, I didn't know if you'd be back at all. Every day I expected to see a For Sale sign go up at your house."

Tyler was stunned to discover she wasn't kidding. "Why would you think that?"

"You took Missy with you!"

He frowned uncomprehendingly for an instant. Then his mouth quirked. "Sam was upset, huh?"

"She was crushed when she found out you took her," Cass admitted. "She thought you should have left her with us, but then she was afraid you were mad at her."

Tyler shook his head. "That wasn't it at all. And I would have left Missy with you, if I'd been thinking straight when I left."

"I know." Cass laughed nervously. "But by then I was worried, too, especially since I knew it was me you were angry with. And then I decided I might have driven you away...." She was babbling. She knew it, but there didn't seem to be a thing she could do about it.

"Cass." The dish towel was pulled from her hands and tossed aside. Warm hands settled upon her bare shoulders. "Honey, look at me."

Her eyes squeezed shut. She couldn't. She was suddenly quaking inside. Afraid this was all a dream, and if she opened her eyes, he would disappear.

Tyler bent forward, pushed aside her hair and kissed the side of her neck, the gentle curve of her cheek. Lips that were incredibly tender sipped away the scalding tear that escaped beneath the closed eyelids.

His breath fanned her cheek. "Silly woman," he chided gently. "I'm here because this is where I belong. Because it's the only place in the world I want to be. Ever." He kissed her trembling mouth. "I love you," he whispered, his voice so achingly tender it brought fresh tears. "Today. Tomorrow. Forever."

With his touch, all her doubt—all her fears—slipped away. She opened her eyes. The heartfelt emotion on his face made her believe in the pot of gold at the end of the rainbow. But it was more than enough right now to simply believe in him, in the raw conviction she heard in his voice.

"Tyler." With a strangled cry, she flung herself against him. "Oh, Tyler, I love you, too."

Tyler's heart contracted with pure, sweet pleasure. His laugh was as shaky as her voice. "Something tells me I'd better make the most of this."

The laughter faded from his expression; the burning intensity that replaced it made her catch her breath.

His eyes searched hers. "I don't think I could stand it if I asked you to marry me again and you refused...."

"Ask me," she pleaded raggedly.

His eyes darkened. "I thought I'd go crazy this last week."

"I was miserable, too," she confided breathlessly.

"I could never hurt you and the kids the way Rick did. Never, Cass, do you hear?" His hands stole up to cradle her face, his voice low and urgent. His gaze seared hers, demanding that she understand. "I'm not like him, not at all...."

"I know that. I think I knew it all along. It just took me a while to finally admit it to myself." And now that she had, she prayed it wasn't too late. "*Now* will you ask me?"

Her wobbly smile made Tyler's heart turn over. His thumbs traced winged patterns on her cheeks. "I want to be your husband, Cass. Your lover and your friend. I want to adopt the kids and be a real father to them." He paused for a second. "I love you. Will you marry me?"

She stared at him, unable to speak for the huge lump in her throat. Nor did she care if her heart was in her eyes. "Yes!" she cried at last, almost choking. "Oh, yes!"

The words acted like a release on a floodgate. He dragged her against him. Cass was certain she would burst with the joy that claimed her as their lips met and clung. But there was time for only a single, lingering kiss.

The front screen slammed again and there was a rush of footsteps. Tyler raised his head just as Katie appeared in the doorway. Trailing behind were her three siblings.

"Oops! Wrong turn, guys!" At the sight of her mother wrapped in Tyler's arms, Katie started to do an abrupt about-face. Tyler stopped her just in time.

"Don't leave yet," he said over the top of Cass's head. "The four of you are just the ones we wanted to see."

Katie turned slowly. Todd peeked around her. "Doesn't look like it to me," he snickered.

"Oh, but you are," Tyler said mildly. He pulled Cass around and anchored her to his side, an arm around her shoulders. He glanced at Todd, brows upraised. "How would you feel about another man in the house, young man?"

Todd blinked, his expression as baffled as Samantha and Trisha's. Katie squealed, her eyes flying to her mother. "He asked you to marry him, didn't he?"

Tyler chuckled. Cass threaded the fingers of her right hand through Tyler's, where it rested on her shoulder. "Yes," she murmured. "He did." She smiled, melding her gaze warmly with Tyler's.

Sam and Trisha exchanged looks, their eyes wide as saucers. Katie merely grinned. Todd's jaw dropped. "Did you say yes?"

Cass nodded, looking from one small face to the other. "You don't mind, do you?"

"Mind!" Katie sang out. "Are you kidding?"

Until now, Todd had appeared rather stunned. "Hey," he said suddenly. His gaze encompassed his three sisters. "If we lived at Tyler's house, you could all have your own bedrooms. And we'd be able to go swimming every day in our very own backyard!"

"Well," Cass said and chuckled. "Tyler's house *is* bigger—"

"Correction." Tyler squeezed her shoulder. "*Our* house."

Sam planted herself squarely in front of Tyler, her eyes rounded with excitement. "What about Missy? Would Missy be our dog, too?"

Tyler slipped his free arm around the little girl and pulled her close, his expression so incredibly soft that Cass found herself fighting tears all over again. "Yeah," he said softly, then teased. "And I think Missy knew it even before the rest of us."

Trisha tugged at his shirt, gazing up at him earnestly. "If Mommy marries you, would you be my dad then?"

He withdrew his arm from Cass and eased himself down so he was on the same level with Trisha. "Yes, I would," he answered gravely. "Would you like that?"

Trisha threw herself against him and wrapped her arms around his neck.

Tyler's laugh was shaky. "I guess that makes the decision unanimous." He marveled at how things had changed since the days these four youngsters had nearly scared him off. Now he only felt proud and humble that they would accept him into their family so freely.

Samantha was beaming. "I'm gonna go tell Missy." She darted from the kitchen, Trisha right behind her.

Katie grinned at her brother. "Maybe we should leave before these two boot us out of here."

Cass merely shook her head. "Sometimes you're just a little too wise for your own good, young lady."

"If that were true, I'd offer to take Todd, Sam and Trisha to the new Walt Disney movie downtown, so certain people could have a little time alone." Her smile was innocence itself. "It's a double feature, too."

Tyler groaned. "Why do I have the feeling this is going to cost me?"

Katie laughed. "Double my allowance and we'll be on the next bus downtown."

She didn't complain when Tyler informed her he'd take the matter up with her mother—but much later. In less than fifteen minutes, he and Cass watched them pile onto the bus at the corner.

Tyler wasted no time slipping his arm around her and guiding their steps in the direction of his house—or rather, their house. Scant seconds later they stood in the middle of the bedroom, arms wrapped loosely around each other.

Cass rubbed her cheek against his shoulder, loving the feel of muscle and bone.

"Cass." Her name emerged as a low wisp of sound. She raised her head.

His touch infinitely gentle, he brushed her lips with his. "You know I'll always be here for you," he whispered.

A purely feminine thrill shot through her. She loved the way his eyes caressed her. They filled her vision, her soul, her world.

"I know," she said softly, then paused. She toyed with a button on his shirt, feeling inexplicably shy. "Did you really mean it? About adopting the kids?"

He captured her hand and brought it to his mouth. Holding her gaze, he kissed her palm. "Yes," he said huskily. He was smiling, but his eyes were serious as they searched hers. "I love them, Cass. Not just because they're a part of you, but because of who they are." He smiled. "I'm going to love being married to you, lady."

She smiled against his mouth. "And I know why, too. Because you won't have to do your own cooking anymore."

His slow-growing grin was wickedly suggestive, wickedly delightful. "I can think of a few other compensations, too.... Which reminds me—" bold and daring fingertips trespassed below the neckline of her blouse "—why don't we take a nice, leisurely dip in the Jacuzzi for a while? After that, who knows...?"

It wasn't long before silken, bubbling water enveloped them both. "I still think this bathroom is utterly decadent." Her tongue flicked at a crystal drop of water sparkling among the golden down on his chest.

"It's certainly had an influence on you," he teased.

"But I suppose it's only fitting we should end up here." She sighed. "After all, this is where it all started...."

He reached for her. Her smug laugh turned to a moan when he pulled her close and took her mouth in a long, drugging kiss. He released her lips and nuzzled the baby-soft skin below her ear. His chuckle was low and husky. "I feel it's only fair to warn you, soon-to-be-wife, that this is only the beginning."

He was right, she realized as love swelled deep inside her. He was hers and she was his. Today. Tomorrow.

Forever.

This month's irresistible novels from
— Temptation —

A MILLION REASONS WHY by Ruth Jean Dale

Marry rich, that was what Mimi Carlton was determined to do. She had a plan and when she kissed millionaire Dusty McLain she thought all her wishes had come true. Dusty liked to keep his relationships simple – purely sexual – until he met Mimi. But then he learned of her vow. . .

UNWILLING WIFE by Renee Roszel

Gina Baron was sick and tired of being her husband's perfect little wife. She had had enough of David's domineering control of her life. So Gina filed for divorce and moved away. Now she was *free*. But just how free was she? Especially after David showed up, as darkly handsome and devastatingly sexy as ever.

LIKE A LOVER by Sandra James

Cass Lawrence's new neighbour made quite an impression when he rescued her four children from a fire in her home. But Cass knew from experience that men weren't really heroes. So why should sexy Tyler Grant keep assuming that role in her dreams?

THE LADY AND THE DRAGON by Regan Forest

Dragons were the stuff of legends, and Prince Charming existed only in fairy tales. Despite her romantic inclinations, Katherine Glenn knew that was reality. Until she came to visit Michael Reese in his castle in Wales. Then reality blurred with fantasy. . .

PRESENT
THE 50TH ROMANCE BY
JESSICA STEELE
'DESTINED TO MEET'

Popular Romance author Jessica Steele finds her inspiration by travelling extensively and researching her backgrounds. But she hates to leave her delightfully soppy Staffordshire Bull Terrier, Daisy, behind, and likes nothing better than to work in her study overlooking a beautiful Worcestershire valley, backed by a hill and a long stretch of trees – "an ideal spot for writing" she says.

You're sure to agree when you read her latest intriguing love story *'Destined to Meet'* – don't miss it!

Published: October 1992   Price: £1.70

Available from Boots, Martins, John Menzies, W.H. Smith,
most supermarkets and other paperback stockists.
Also available from Mills & Boon Reader Service, PO Box 236,
Thornton Road, Croydon, Surrey CR9 3RU.